Angela DiMarco Lombardo makes her own decisions. The independent widow is headstrong and ruthless. Manipulating anyone who stands in her way. She doesn't care whose heart she has to tread on to achieve her goals.

Billionaire playboyAndre Bourbon, maybe ten years younger than Angela, but that doesn't stop her from manipulating him. Luring him with false desire and empty promises of sizzling nights of passion.

The pleasure seeking billionaire playboy, is enraged when he learns how thoroughly deceived he was by Angela and how she used him. Playing him for a fool in more ways than one. He is consumed with rage.

Kidnapping her from her home in Palermo and holding her captive in his Paris mansion is just the beginning. His blinding rage demands that he must possess the Sicilian beauty at any cost. He won't rest until he owns her body, mind, and soul.

THE FRENCHMAN'S REVENGE

CINDY REDDING

With love for my family

CHAPTER 1

ecember 20. Palermo, Sicily

ANDRE BOURBON STEPPED out of the backseat of the sleek silver Mercedes limousine, buttoned the top button of his gray Armani suit, and turned to his driver.

"James, wait in the car. I'm not sure how long I'll be."

"Yes, sir."

Andre removed his black-framed sunglasses and pushed his blond hair back from his brow. He looked up at the three-story stone townhouse in an upscale residential area in Palermo. The second and third floors had Juliet balconies and on the balconies were some terra-cotta pots brimming with rosemary and lavender. The green-painted wood shutters were open to allow the morning light in.

Shouts of laughter could be heard from the lush park across the way. The weather was mild for December, and the Sicilian sun shone brightly, like a big slice of lemon against the cloudless azure sky.

He'd arrived in Palermo on his private jet early this morning from his villa in Parma. Less than twenty-four hours ago, he'd learned how Angela DiMarco Lombardo, deceitful seductress with an angel's face, had used him in a game of betrayal. It irked him, eating at his gut since he found out how he'd been played. He'd been manipulated from the beginning—five years ago—Angela persuaded him to meet her nephew Ricardo DiMarco, the CEO of DiMarco Enterprises, and his mistress Liz Ferguson. Now, all these years later, the pieces fell into place.

First thing this morning, he met with Gianni DiMarco, corporate counsel for DiMarco Enterprises, at their Palermo headquarters. Andre released his interests in the Contessa Line cruise ship's stocks, signing the proxies over to Ricardo yesterday. That lying bitch Angela had cajoled him into purchasing those stocks. His name was on the certificates, but with money she'd given him. Now, the money for the stocks had been transferred to his account for a little over two million dollars. Andre would keep that money, although he certainly didn't need any of it. He was a man who knew the ins and outs of corporate acquisitions. He ran a corporation just as impressive as DiMarco Enterprises. His company had offices around the world and interests in many various enterprises, and yet he'd been duped by a sweet-faced devious beauty.

Yesterday, when Ricardo had come to his villa, Andre realized how he'd been used by Angela from the beginning of their friendship. He knew without a doubt why, and the more he thought about it, the angrier he became. Angela had set him up with a woman who resembled Liz. They had a one-night stand, and he was unaware that they took photos of him and the woman having sex. He would find Angela, that deceitful bitch, and make her pay for using him. That was his plan. His eyes narrowed. Here he stood on the front steps of that lying, scheming manipulator's home.

He composed himself before he rang the doorbell, making a conscious effort to unclench his jaw.

"Chi e´," her sweet voice came over the intercom.

"Ciao, Angela, *sono io* Andre Bourbon." He kept his voice calm; no sense alerting the viper of his anger.

The buzzer sounded, unlocking the entry. A smile crossed his lips as he noticed the keyless entry system. He opened the heavy green-painted, wood-carved front door. Andre stepped into a neat foyer onto a round rug in vivid colors of yellow and red, with splashes of bright blues and greens like the colors in the famous *Carretto Siciliano*. Marble stairs sat directly in front of him and on the right, a door led to the garage.

Like most townhomes in Europe, the kitchen, dining room, and living room were on the top floor, with a large rooftop terrace above it. The bedrooms and den were on the second floor and on the first, an entry and garage access. Hers was no different. He glanced around, an oil painting depicting Mount Etna with its snow-covered mountaintop and smoke pluming up from the volcano hung on the wall. A table against one wall held a Murano glass vase filled with silk flowers, and beside the vase a set of car keys and mail.

He climbed the steps, admiring the decor and the choice of paintings hanging on the wall. On the second-floor landing, another accent table covered with a crocheted doily, a Capodimonte figurine sat in the center. On the landing walls, several more oil paintings hung. He glanced down the hall before climbing to the third floor.

Angela stood at the top of the landing in her signature widow black. Her black hair tied on top of her head into an old lady's bun, a hint of red on her lips. The A-line mourning black dress had long, fitted sleeves and a modest scoop neck.

The hem of the dress reached just below her knees. Low-heel pumps, naturally in black, finished her outfit. Around her neck, a string of pearls and on her ears, the matching pearl earrings.

Her dark-as-night eyes looked at him in surprise. "How are you? Please come in… but you know we shouldn't be seen together before our little venture is complete. I'm surprised to see you here."

I'll bet you are. "I happened to be in Palermo on business, and I couldn't go without saying hello to my favorite Sicilian widow."

He stepped onto the landing, and Angela reached up to kiss him first on his right cheek and then on his left, in the Italian tradition. She was petite and needed to rise on her toes while he bent his six-feet three-inch frame to her and inhaled the light-orange-blossom scent of her perfume.

"This is quite a surprise. It's too early for *pranso*, but would you like a coffee?"

"Yes, coffee would be great." He looked around the house as she led him to a cozy and inviting living room. A sofa upholstered in jade-green silk faced two cream-colored accent chairs, and an oval coffee table stood between. Placed on the highly polished wood was a Murano glass dish filled with chocolate candy. He glanced around, admiring the great artwork that hung on the walls.

"Please sit. I'll be right back with the coffee."

Andre walked around the living room. Everything was neat and tidy. Then he went over to the window and glanced out. *Good, James parked the car by the garage.* He glanced into the dining room. The dining table gleamed with a coat of fresh polish; around the table were six tall-back chairs, with the seats upholstered in a light green watered silk fabric. In the corner, he spotted a mini bar.

He stood near the sofa when she walked back in, carrying

a sterling-silver tray with a china espresso pot, two china cups and saucers, along with a sugar bowl, all in the same design. Two white-linen napkins and sterling-silver demitasse spoons. She put the tray on the coffee table by the sofa. "Please come sit with me." Her delicate hand patted the sofa near where she'd sat. Then she poured the coffee into both cups. "Tell me, I can't seem to remember. Do you take sugar in your coffee?"

"I like my coffee sweet like you, Angela." He'd always flirted with her, and she'd promised him more than flirting once the agreement they'd made was complete. Her head snapped up, and he chuckled. "Do you have any Sambuca?"

"*Si*, you want *un caffe corretto*. I will be right back." She walked into the dining room, and Andre slipped a small vial from his jacket pocket and poured the powder into Angela's cup.

When he'd learned what she'd done, he was furious with himself for underestimating her deceitful, vindictive ways. She was diabolical, the way she played him like a fool, using him in her plan to destroy her nephew Ricardo DiMarco and his lover Liz Ferguson. Andre had no idea what Angela was capable of with that sweet, innocent face of hers. He'd been attracted to her from the moment they'd met years earlier, although he had closed himself off to love. Sex was always an option.

He'd never told anyone that he'd lost his wife and all their dreams when she'd succumbed to a terrible disease seven years ago, and since that time, he'd been vulnerable. No serious relationships. He'd never find the kind of love he'd had with his wife. She'd been his life and then in the blink of an eye, it was over.

Angela had been different. She was older than he by ten years. She'd flirted with him, and he would have liked to date her—go to bed with her.

They never connected, and she'd gone to live in New York with her nephew Ricardo. She'd asked him for a favor, and he couldn't refuse. She'd made it sound so innocent. "Oh, you should go on this cruise, although you probably own a yacht. My nephew and his flavor of the month Liz Ferguson will be on board." Then last year, she asked him if he could buy stocks for her, "but, please, for my sake you must keep them in your name." She pressed him for this tiny favor and agreed to a sexual relationship once the deal was complete. "After the shareholders' meeting in January, I will stay with you for as long as you like."

Now he kept his fury in check. Picking up his cup, he watched Angela as she stirred her coffee and then, in two dainty sips, she finished her drink, placing the empty cup on her saucer. He wouldn't allow himself the satisfaction of a smile. "So, what have you been up to recently? I haven't talked with you in months."

"I've been so very busy. Some of the family had come to New York for a holiday shopping spree and the theater. I've just returned home… a few days ago. Now, I'm getting ready for Christmas. I don't know if you're aware, but Giorgio bought a new vineyard in California in the Napa Valley. He'd come to New York for a while before going there. He was lucky to have missed the blizzard that stranded most of us in New York City."

"You have been busy. Where will you spend the holiday season?"

"I'll be here in Palermo with my brother and sister-in-law. They'll do all the entertaining, which is great. I only have to make an appearance. Then on New Year's Eve, my nephew Gianni, Ricardo's brother, is getting married."

She should only know I met with Gianni earlier today. "I have an apartment in New York, and the corporate headquarters of my latest acquisition is on Lexington Avenue." He picked up his cup and drank the coffee down in one shot. "Perhaps next time we are both in New York, we can go to dinner and the theater."

She stood and faced him, her eyes flashing. "Why did you come here, Andre? You know we shouldn't be seen together before the DiMarco Enterprises shareholders meeting in New York." She laughed at him. "Do you think that I would lower myself to date a man who is only five years older than my son?"

He noticed for the first time how beautiful she was—her flawless complexion, the curve of her jaw. Heat settled in his groin. "Oh Angel, we did agree to have a relationship, but if you don't want my attention... I'm not hurt. I do want you to know what you'll be missing." He was quick. Standing up before his words had a chance to register, he grabbed Angela in one fluid motion. Andre held her upper arm and spun her around into his arms. Her lips parted in surprise, and he took full advantage. Dragging her hips into his body, he devoured her mouth, wanting to suck the very breath from her.

Andre was a tall, broad-shouldered man, and she was so petite. He dragged her delicate wrists behind her back, clasping them in one hand at the base of her spine. He held her body to him. Bending her back, his tongue sparred with hers as she tried to release her mouth from his. She stomped on the arch of his Italian leather-shod foot. He pulled her fully into his body, his knee between her legs. He wouldn't allow her to escape.

She wretched her mouth away enough to hiss, "You bastard, let me go."

"No, never. I'm going to fuck you until you beg me to never let you go."

"You don't get it. You're young enough to be my son."

"Not unless you were ten." He released her wrists, and she pushed at his shoulders.

He lifted Angela higher against his body. "Stop struggling, wildcat. I know you want me."

"No, I don't. Let me go." She pummeled his chest. "Oh," she groaned, and her lids slowly slipped over her coal-black eyes. She stopped resisting and blinked. "I... what?" She gazed into his eyes.

One of his brows rose.

She struggled to keep her eyes open. "Andre, what... did... you... do?" She passed out in his arms.

A slow smile crept across his lips. He laid her on the sofa and then took the tray with the coffee to the kitchen. He rinsed the cups in the sink, cleaned the espresso pot, then dried the cups and pot, replacing them in the cupboard where he'd watched her take them from.

Andre hurried down the stairs to her bedroom. Opening the armoire, he grabbed a handful of clothes. His brow furrowed, and he shook his head. *All she owns are black outfits.* He threw them into a suitcase he found in her closet. On her dresser was a wedding photo in an ornate gold frame of a young Angela and a handsome man with dark hair and aqua-blue eyes. Next to that was a photo of Angela holding an infant. *Probably her son, Giorgio.* There were other framed photos. Andre closed the suitcase and left it on the landing near the steps.

Then he went back upstairs and grabbed her cell phone from the kitchen table where he saw it earlier. Andre scrolled through her contacts until he found her son Giorgio's number. He texted a message, making sure it went through, then powered off her phone. He shoved it into his suit pants pocket and glanced around, checking that everything was in place and undisturbed.

Andre called his driver. "I'll be right down with a guest. Wait by the side entrance to the garage." He ended the call, picked up Angela's limp form, and headed downstairs. On the second-floor landing, he grabbed her suitcase and went down to the garage and out the back door. That door automatically locked, so anyone who came looking for her would think she'd left on her own. He was wise to her now, and his plan would be flawless. Her red Fiat remained in the garage, but anyone looking for her would assume she'd taken a taxi to the airport or to the train station.

His driver took the suitcase from him and put it in the limousine's trunk. Andre laid Angela in the backseat and slipped in next to her, holding her head on his lap. "Did you call the airport, James?"

"Yes, sir. Your plane is ready for immediate departure."

Andre relaxed against the leather seat. The drive to the airport would take less than ten minutes. He turned his attention to the unconscious woman lying across his lap. Her hair had come loose from that ridiculous bun. He could see the black strands were long and shiny. He ran his fingers through the silky mass. She wore no makeup other than the slight tint on her lips. Her olive skin was flawless, without wrinkles, and her long black lashes rested on her cheeks. Angela's full bottom lip had a slight indent in the center, and the top lip was a perfect bow. Sleeping, she looked sweet and innocent. No one would ever suspect her devious nature.

They arrived at his jet. Andre carried her through the cabin and laid her on his bed. She would sleep through the flight and, if he were lucky, until they arrived at his home in Paris.

CHAPTER 2

There wasn't just one thing that attacked Angela's senses when she suddenly came around. Her arms were spread wide above her head, with each wrist tied with soft fabric, stopping her from moving. The gag in her mouth prevented her from screaming, and the blindfold terrified her.

She lay still—

"Ahh, I see you're finally awake."

She recognized that French drawl. Andre! Angela squirmed against the ties.

"I'm not done, wildcat." He grasped her ankle with his strong fingers.

She pulled against the ties while she tried to talk around the gag. "Ahh… mmm… ah."

"No, *bellissima*, I don't want to hear anything, especially your lies." He finished tying her right ankle, and she felt his fingers close over her other ankle. He dragged it, spreading her legs apart. She tried to kick at him.

He laughed. "You think I'd allow you to hurt me."

She struggled, yanking on her arms and legs. In that terrifying moment, she realized she was naked.

"I secured you to the bed, and now you cannot get away." Fear burst into her brain. She couldn't see him. He stroked a hand up her leg, his fingers trailing along her inner thigh, lingering at the juncture of her legs. "You have a beautiful body, Angela. You've kept it well hidden, with oversized black clothes… When was the last time you fucked?"

She shook her head violently, yanking on her arms. Spread-eagled as she was, she couldn't move her legs.

He laughed. "You cannot escape me. I'll have my revenge on your body. I'm delightfully surprised… You have a thirty-four-year-old son, yet your body looks like that of a thirty-year-old." His hand glided up her abdomen, over her torso, and he cupped her breast. "Your tits are firm, no sag here." Playing with a nipple, he rotated it with his fingers. "Oh, is that too much?" he said.

Her head moved from side to side as she screamed around the gag.

His hot breath touched her breasts as he spoke, "So, no?"

When his tongue circled her nipple, she did scream, moving to get away. He wouldn't relent. She groaned at the zap of desire that flew through her, tightening her nipple.

Andre snickered and continued to play with her breasts. He stroked her stomach before his hand moved along her belly.

She tingled.

Then his palm glided back up to her other breast, molding her in his hand. "What a surprise to find that your tits are perfection—big but not overly large." His breath was warm on her breasts. He sucked her nipple into his mouth, his tongue pressing and coaxing. Her libido awoke.

When was the last time she felt this way? *Oh God, now*

what? He slid his hand down the center of her belly, moving lower and lower, between her spread legs. *Oh, please don't.* One finger moved into her, touching her clitoris. She yelled into the gag.

"I see I'll have to work a little to make you wet." He pulled his finger out of her.

She struggled against the ties, trying to move her arms, and kicked her feet in a futile effort to get away from him.

Andre laughed again; his deep voice held no mercy. "Let me see… I'm sure… I can make you beg and not push away from me."

The bed dipped.

What was he up to? Oh, no! His lips brushed against her nipple, and he sucked it into his mouth. Fire touched her. His tongue glided over and over her nipple until it tightened into a stiff peak. *Oh, God.* He massaged her other breast, cupping and molding it to his desire.

She willed herself not to feel, crave, ache as his lips continued to suck and nibble. He plucked at her breast, teasing her, then squeezed the nipple between his fingers. She groaned as her flesh tightened with a burning zing of desire.

He said with triumph, "Ahh, not too much work."

Blindfolded and gagged, all she could do was feel what he would do next as his hand moved down her body. Angela fought her own desire and tried to stop feeling. She hadn't been with anyone but her husband, and he had been dead for twenty-five years!

Andre left her breasts. She almost sighed in relief, but then her stomach tightened as his hand moved along her skin to the juncture of her spread legs. She pulled against the ties at her ankles.

He touched her between her spread legs, pressing a finger

into her vagina and swirling it around. "Still dry. I have to work a little harder, but you know I'm a patient man."

He made her nervous as he slid his long middle finger deep into her. She willed her mind to relax, but that only made it worse. Now she could feel everything he was doing. *O Dio mio.*

His long, masculine finger went deeper into her vagina, touching nerve endings that hadn't been alive in twenty-five years. Andre pulled out, then pushed in deeper than before, resting his palm against her mound. His breath touched her breast, and he blew on her wet nipple.

Ahh.

He was relentless as he slid his finger in, laying his palm against her as he swirled that finger deep in her core. Then he crooked the pad of that finger over a spot that made her heart thump erratically before pulling out, only to thrust in again. In and out of her, over and over. *Ahh, Santo Cielo Ahh. What he is doing so... so very, o... Dio mio.*

With the next stroke, he touched her clitoris, waking feelings that her celibate existence had long forgotten. He traced her nipple with the tip of his tongue before he licked the peak and sucked her nipple deep into his mouth.

She couldn't move away. He pushed a second finger into her quivering vagina and sucked her nipple into his mouth, lathing it with his tongue. Her heart pounded. He touched her clitoris again, slowly pushed his fingers deep into her, and then slowly slid both out. In and out, twice more. She fought against the feelings he ignited.

"Yes, Angela, nice. You're getting slick. Good." His French-accented voice dripped satisfaction.

Slowly, he slid both his fingers into her vagina, holding them deep in her core, then he scissored them into her before he leisurely slid them out. "Now, you're nice and wet.

Good, *bien*. I knew you could get my fingers ready to fuck you."

She heard the sneer in his voice, adding to her own humiliation. Angela kept her lower body as still as she could. She tried to scream, curse at him, but the damn gag prevented her. *O Dio, Dio, Dio.*

His fingers moved in her, stretching her, pushing in and out. He stroked up her cleft to her clitoris, bringing the nerve endings to life.

Angela held her breath as he played with her. Andre used her own desire against her. His slick fingers tormented her until the need to lift her hips almost overwhelmed her. *No, no, no!* She tried to hold still, biting on the gag, forcing herself not to move.

She wanted this, yes… No, she did not. Then she couldn't stop herself. She needed to move. She couldn't control the urge any longer, and she tipped her pelvis up, needing more of his long, thick fingers. He moved them into her vagina. *Ahhh, si ahh, ahh, si, si.*

He slid his fingers out of her, and she tried to lift herself to him, wanting him to go deeper. The blindfold prevented her from seeing him. In her mind's eye, she saw him as he always was—handsome with his blond hair and distinct pewter eyes.

His tongue lashed at her nipple. With his soft breath on her aching nipple, he said, "Good. Are you ready to come? I can feel you all wound up. Your pussy is quivering… I think… I'll take a break… I'm tired."

He moved from her. His weight left the bed.

She was glad, she told herself, breathing a sigh of relief.

"You look like the slut you are. You should see your pussy dripping wet now. My fingers have your scent on them. Here, smell yourself." He put his hand near her nose. She turned her head away. "Oh, you don't like that? I think after I make you come, I'll remove the gag so you can taste yourself. What do you think? *Bien?*"

She turned away from him, yelling into the material.

Angela couldn't see him and banished the image she'd conjured up of his handsome face from her mind. She wanted him to go. She groaned into the gag as the bed dipped again. He was at her side. Andre played with her once again, his tongue circling her nipple and licking until it drew tight. He licked and licked, stroking her other breast in the palm of his powerful hand, until she arched her back, lifting her breast up, offering herself to his mouth.

Her head rolled from side to side on the pillow. Now she was beginning to—Oh God, she hadn't had sex in all these years. The tightness in her abdomen, dragging her hips up, and the burning pleasure between her legs. *Ahh, ahh, yes.*

He brought her to the brink of pleasure just by touching her breasts. The coil in her abdomen tightened; she tilted her pelvis, needing something to fill the empty void. He stopped.

She groaned into the gag, almost screaming.

He laughed. Then he untied the gag.

"You dirty bastard, release me. Take this blindfold off. Let me see your ugly face. I'll—"

"Oh, you're feisty." The gag was back on. "I'm going to enjoy taming you." She screamed into the cloth. Andre laughed louder. "I'm going to suck your nipples. Then…you'll feel what else I suck."

He did, playing with her breasts. Her nipples were tight, raw, but oh so good. He moved down her body, his tongue tracing a path of fire on her abdomen. Her legs spread, and her ankles tied to the corners of the bed. He was between her thighs, holding her. Cupping her mound, his palm rubbed over her. He slipped his big hands under Angela. Holding her buttocks, he squeezed her flesh with his long fingers, massaging her. His thumbs pressed on her seam, and he spread her wide. The slight coolness was so erotic, she didn't have time to think. His lips brushed against her. His tongue moved over her clitoris with feather-light touches.

She screamed into her gag, yanking on her arms and jerking her legs. He brushed his lips against her again and again. He touched her clitoris with more than the tip of his tongue.

She was wound so tight. No, no, she shook her head back and forth. She couldn't move. Then he held her open to his mouth. What was he doing? He sucked her before his tongue traced her most intimate part, and he lapped at her... *Oh. Oh.*

Now she was grateful that she couldn't move her legs, and she couldn't talk. Angela knew she would beg him to continue. He held her heated, excited flesh between his lips, and he did what he said he would. The slight tugging pressure sent shards of wonderful desire through her. Her head pressed back into the pillow, and the gag cut off her moan of pleasure.

His tongue joined the attack, lingering on the spot that gave her the most unbearable pleasure. Oh God—he sucked, her body tensed, and she was getting primed for a huge orgasm. He brought her to a point where she wanted every dirty thing he said he would do. Her abdomen muscles tightened, and her head pushed back into the pillow, arching her back. She panted into the gag.

He stopped.

"Agh," she groaned.

Now she wished the gag were off so she could beg and plead with him to make her come. Surely, she would go insane if he didn't finish.

Once more, he left the bed.

Her blood sizzled through her. Her clit was on fire, needing him to finish. Her breath heaved through her chest.

Then slowly, she relaxed. She was in control of her body once again. Had he left the room?

The scent of his spicy cologne drifted around her, and the mattress dipped with his tall frame. He'd come back. She groaned when he kissed her body again, running his tongue on her inner thighs, holding her open so he could thrust his tongue into her repeatedly. It didn't take long for Angela to lift her pelvis, offering herself to his mouth.

He stopped.

Ohhhh, I hate him.

He lay next to her, his hand stroking her belly. She panted as his hand moved lower and lower, drawing patterns on her sensitized flesh.

His velvet-edged voice held a trace of anger. "I know you set me up." His French accent sent a shiver up her spine as he whispered near her ear, "Your nephew Ricardo came to my villa in Parma. He brought all the dirty pictures you gave him."

She jerked her head away; the gag muffled her scream, her brain racing. *He knows what I did!*

"Oh, don't scream." His voice dropped to a sexy whisper, "I'm going to make you moan in pleasure, not pain." He dipped his long finger into her, then thrust deep, swirling it in her vagina. "You're nice and wet now… dripping wet." He stopped and then moved to the foot of the bed, wedging his body between her legs. "You know what I'm going to do now?"

She hoped he would do what he had said. *Yes, yes.* His tongue slipped around her clitoris. Not even her husband had done this. She knew there were men who did. *Oh, oh.* She pulled against her restraints, not to pull away but to hold him closer to her. Andre's hands slid under her buttocks, lifting her. *What is he doing?* Exposed to his lips and tongue, his hands lifted her to his mouth. *Oh. No. No. No... Yes... Yes... Yes, ahh yes.*

Then he stopped.

"Agh." She struggled against her restraints, now with an aching need for him to make her come. She was stronger than this.

Through the haze of desire, she heard his husky whisper, "What do you think? Shall I make you come? I like this, you not being able to answer. Your pussy is telling me. Maybe I'll make you beg me."

This time, she didn't know what he did. He rose up her body. She realized he was naked as his warm flesh moved over her. His muscular thighs spread on either side of her ribs.

"Ricardo brought me all the photos." He stopped talking as his knees hugged her torso, and the palm of his hand caressed her cheek. "I won't hurt you." The gentleness of his voice surprised her. A heartbeat later, he held her breasts in his big hands, rubbing her nipples with his thumbs. "Your tits are perfect for this."

She almost stopped breathing when Andre lay his erect shaft in the valley of her breasts. He held her breasts in his two powerful hands, molding them around his erection. He stroked himself with her. "I would like you to suck my dick, but we'll have to wait for that."

Mortified, lying tied to the bed, Angela couldn't think.

He moved his steel-hard shaft between her breasts, his hands molding her around him. His massive thigh muscles held her as he pushed his hips, her cleavage giving him friction as he slid himself back and forth between the valley of her breasts. There was no pain, just humiliation.

"I thought you were the perfect woman. I would have treasured you, but all you did was use me, manipulate me. Where did you find that woman who looked so much like

Ricardo's woman? How were you able to get photos of us?" He stroked himself between her breasts as he spoke, "Do you know which photo he showed me first?"

Angela groaned into the gag, shaking her head.

"She was on her knees, and my dick was in her mouth." Andre held her breasts tighter around his hard flesh as he stroked against her. "Before we're finished, I'll do the same and more with you." He pressed her breasts around him, rubbing her nipples with his thumbs.

"Should I take the blindfold off so you can see what I'm doing?"

She shook her head.

"No? But why? This is only the beginning, my sweet Angela." He stopped talking as he held her breasts together around his penis. His massive thighs gripped her. He moved faster, straddling her, his cock resting in her cleavage as he thrust his hips forward, with short, quick moves back and forth. His breathing became labored. He groaned. His erection throbbed in the valley of her breasts. She'd never felt anything so erotic and unexpected.

"Ahh," he shouted. Moving faster, he used her like a… like a slut.

She couldn't see what he did next, but he must have gotten a handkerchief to spill his seed in. Angela felt the cloth as he jerked a few more times, then he got off her and left her in her shame.

She didn't know that he could do something like that. Was there a photo of him doing that with the other woman? She hadn't looked at all the pictures; she just sent them to Ricardo. She hoped Andre was done, but then she wrenched away from his hands. He'd come back silently.

"Are your breasts sore?"

She thought for a moment and realized they weren't, but

she wouldn't answer him. All she wanted was to curse him and his whole family.

"Let me kiss them and make them better."

Oh, no. No more. He kissed, massaged, and sucked at her breasts until she thought she would die. Something happened. She felt heaviness between her legs, deep in her vagina. She was wet and on fire. She shattered, climaxing with him touching her nipples.

"Oh, you're going to be the best whore. You're so responsive. I've heard that some women can come like this. It pleases me immensely that you're one of them."

With her last shudder, he slid down between her spread legs and rubbed her mound. "You're very, very wet; the sheet between your lovely legs is soaked with your creamy juices." He stroked his finger into her, deeper and deeper, searching for what she didn't know. He licked her clit while he crooked his finger. "How does that feel?"

O... h... ahh. Her body sizzled on overload. She was alive with so many feelings. Then suddenly, raw, hot waves of blissful pleasure shot through her. Arching her back, she screamed into the gag.

"Oh, so good," he said as he continued to thrust two fingers into her. "You're... coming again... so hot." He stopped talking as she pulsed around his fingers. When her spasms slowed, he waited for the last shudder of her orgasm before he stroked into her again and again.

She was on fire. Her clit throbbed against his thumb as her vagina pulsed around the strokes of his long fingers. Three more times, he used his fingers to make her climax.

She didn't care anymore; she just felt. He didn't remove the blindfold or the gag. She must have fallen asleep. She woke up to him kissing her. How could she have dosed off like that? He kissed her neck, her belly, her abdomen, down one leg. *What?*

He'd untied her ankle and held her other. "No kicking," he said. "Or I'll leave this leg tied." He waited until she nodded her head. Then he untied that ankle and kissed up her legs. Reaching her center, she tried to move.

"Oh no, don't, or I'll secure your ankles again."

She relaxed her legs.

"You can lift your knees and wrap yourself around my head." He laughed when she groaned into her gag. Andre kissed her center. "You know you were made for this. For me to touch you here." The here was her core. He stopped talking and kissed her. His tongue was magic, and she didn't want to fight the feelings he evoked in her. With her legs free her feet inched up the mattress, she raised her knees. She was so hot for his mouth, her pelvis tightened, and her hips tilted up, offering him all of her.

She wished her hands were free so she could press him to her, run her fingers through his short, blond hair. She wanted the gag off so she could... What was she saying? Oh God, he was so talented to make her want this. His will became her will, and she didn't know where one ended and the other began.

He moved up her body, and the hardness of his erection rested at her entrance, teasing, rubbing without entering, "I want to see you when I take your hot pussy." He pulled her blindfold off.

She saw his cropped blond hair tousled and disheveled. His sculpted lips—Don't think where those lips were and what he did with them and his tongue. He smiled into her eyes, but his were stormy gray. No, ice cold. Yes, they were... cold after all the intimate things he did. A glint of rage remained in the silver depths.

"The gag stays, but I want to see you the first time I stick my dick in you and fuck you."

She felt him at her entrance. "Oh, don't cringe at my

words. You brought this on yourself. You're so nice and slick, but you're tight, so I'll go slow. I don't want to cause pain. I want you to remember the pleasure… only the pleasure."

Andre entered her with a gentleness she didn't expect, just the head of his enormous erection. He was right. She would remember the pleasure. Slowly, because he was massive. She knew that from when he used her breasts to come, now he was giving her a command.

"Open your legs." His knees spread her thighs. "Yes, bend your knees, lift your legs; that's it." He slipped in a little more. He hitched her leg up with his arm, never taking his eyes from hers.

She was bold, not closing her eyes, gazing deep into his stormy silver-gray ones. Trying to melt the ice, she relaxed against him.

"Good girl… that's it, nice and easy… just a little more." His cock stretched her. He stopped, giving her time to adjust to his size.

She didn't think she could take more of his length.

"Oh… yes, so… tight. So nice. Try to relax." He flexed his hips and slipped in a little more. Andre touched her cheek with gentle fingers. "That's it, relax, Angela. There isn't any pain, is there?"

She closed her eyes.

"Look at me."

She did. His jaw thrust forward. "Is there pain?" His mouth set in a determined line.

She shook her head, then turned away.

"Good." One more thrust, and he pushed in all the way to the hilt of his enormous erection.

She stretched to accommodate Andre's huge male length, longer and thicker than her poor dead husband. *No, don't think of him. He left you alone with a young son.*

Andre didn't move. "Look at me, Angela." He waited for her to gaze up at him. "Shall I begin?"

His handsome, chiseled features, his jaw set in determination. She saw beads of sweat on his forehead. He stayed still, with his sculpted lips pressed together. She was so full of his hugeness, but there wasn't any pain, just a fullness. Angela nodded and slowly moved her leg to his hip.

A smile lifted the corners of his sensuous mouth.

He surrounded her, his abdomen pressed to hers, the feel of him deep in her. He was a handsome man. She'd always fought her attraction to him because of the age difference.

"Yes, that's it… good girl."

Oh. Good girl indeed. She would make him eat his words. *What does he think I am?* Angela had no more time to think.

He moved inside her. Andre pulled out enough to thrust into her, stretching her further to accommodate his glorious thick length. The tight friction had her pulling against the ties that bound her wrists, needing him closer.

Angela moaned into her gag as he rode her. Each short, hard thrust brought pleasure as he sent her reeling. Her leg slid up his muscled flank, over his hip. He thrust deeper and deeper. Andre hooked her knee into the crook of his elbow. She lost herself in his eyes, and her body arched up, her breasts ached with what was it? Oh, his lips. She wanted his lips on her breasts, nipping and sucking her nipples.

Andre must have read her mind, he had to have, because he found a nipple and drew the whole of it into his mouth as he pumped into her, harder and faster. Her inner walls rippled—she was going to come again. He sucked her nipple once more before he threw his head back and locked his elbows, moving deeper. He shifted his hips from side to side, and waves of radiating pleasure toppled her over the edge. She came, screaming her need into her gag as the shudders of her orgasm clutched his hard cock, stroking him into her core.

He laughed.

She didn't care.

Andre let out a shout as the heat of his seed shot into her. He heaved, and his body jerked as he pumped every drop of himself into her, grinding his hips, making her clench and ripple around him. He fell forward but kept all his weight from crushing her. His lips were on her neck, sucking her damp skin. She knew he was leaving his mark on her. Angela didn't care, she wanted that and more.

His ragged breath matched her own as she panted, her heart racing.

He breathed into her ear, "Next time, I'll stick my dick in your hot pussy and fuck you from behind with you on your knees. You'll take all of me into that tight pussy and feel my balls slap against your cunt."

She yelled into her gag, wanting to call him every perverted name she could think of.

He laughed at her, shaking his head. "That's not what you screamed before. That was a scream of pleasure. Don't worry, you'll like all I intend to do to you before I send you home."

Home? For the first time since he had removed the blindfold, she looked around. Her eyes wide, she didn't recognize her surroundings. This wasn't her bedroom or her house. *Oh, dear God, where has he taken me? How?*

"Come, I think you need a bath. A good soak in the tub will make you feel better, then we can eat."

He went into the adjoining room; she heard water turn on. Then she tilted her head and looked out the window. All she could see was the sky, and it was evening. *How long was I unconscious? I made him coffee... oh, that dirty bastard... He must have put something in my cup... how trusting I was. I should have known he would find out what I did. I should have left Palermo after I saw Ricardo with Liz.*

She looked around the overly large room—the walls were tinted blue. The high ceilings with their rich carved moulding gilt gold cherubs in each of the four corners. A cut-crystal chandelier hung from a medallion in the center of the ceiling.

He came back to the bed, naked; his lean body was taut with muscles that shifted under his fair skin as he walked. His bulging biceps drew her gaze, then her eyes traveled down a path of dark-blond hair to his narrow waist, tapering down to—*Oh God, even at rest, he's massive.*

"Your bath is ready. Where are you? Why, you have the pleasure of my hospitality at my Paris home."

Her eyes widened.

"Don't be so surprised. I'll tell you everything… more than you did for me, but first a bath and then some food." He untied her wrists.

She reached up to her mouth, yanking on the fabric. "Why, you filthy—"

His finger wagged in front of her. "No calling names, or I'll think you didn't like my lovemaking."

She sat up, pushing her hair from her face.

He extended his hand. "Here, let me help you. The bed is high."

She shoved his hand from her and stood, a little wobbly at first.

Andre held her upper arm to steady her. "Easy, *ma belle,* my petite beauty… You're truly magnificent. Your body—"

She jerked her arm out of his grasp, spun toward him, and swung her fist at his handsome face. Catching him unaware, she connected with his jaw. "Ouch," she cried. Her hand, arm, and shoulder hurt from the impact.

"Oh, I see your Sicilian is showing," he said as he dragged

her into his tall body, taking her hand to hold behind her back. He caught her other arm to her side. "Careful, wildcat, or I may have to tie you and then bathe you myself."

She stopped struggling. "You wouldn't dare."

"You'll learn that I dare anything I wish. Shall I prove it to you again?"

"No *via*, go. Get out. Let me bathe in peace."

"As you wish, pussycat."

"Don't call me that," she shouted at him. Then she lifted her head and strode into the en suite, ignoring him.

CHAPTER 3

*A*ngela gasped, *Oh my, a tub.* She trailed her fingers in the warm swirling water.

Andre, in all his naked splendor, with his fair skin and short, blond, wildly tousled hair, came to stand in the entry. His muscles rippled as his husky voice reached her like a caress. "Wildcat, that's what you are. Don't be too long, you must be hungry. You missed *pranso*, so I ordered dinner for us."

She looked for something to throw at him. Finding a bar of fragrant soap, she aimed for his head. He ducked out of the way before he turned and left the room. His laughter irked her. Mumbling under her breath, she stepped into the magnificent rectangular black bathtub. The jets from the whirlpool were on, and the water swirled, inviting her into its heat. Thankfully, the glow from the crystal chandelier above the tub was set on low. "Ahh, heaven."

She soaked her body, relaxing against the high rim, allowing the warm water and the jets to soothe her. She dunked the sea sponge into the water and dribbled the water over her arms, enjoying the bath. Before getting out of the tub, she washed her hair. Then she picked up a big, fluffy bath towel from the stool beside the tub, dried herself, and wrapped it around her body, tucking the end between her breasts. She didn't have a comb, nor did she see one on the black granite and gold vanity.

Angela used her fingers to comb through her long, black hair. She was one of the lucky ones who didn't have graying hair. When people found out she was forty-nine, they thought she dyed her hair that jet-black color. She usually tied it into a bun, but now she left her long hair down around her shoulders to dry naturally.

She stood in the middle of the luxurious room, looking for something to wear when Andre walked into the en suite, wearing a gray jacket, a black silk shirt open to the waist, and black slacks. He carried a white robe, trimmed in satin over his arm and dangling from two fingers, he held white satin high-heel boudoir slippers. She raised her brow at him.

"For you, wildcat. Drop the towel." He put the slippers down on the marble floor and then held the robe open for her.

She sneered at him. "You can wear clothes, but this is what I have to wear. It's see through with no coverage at all."

He grinned at her and nodded. "Yes, now you're beginning to understand."

She thought for a moment; he saw parts of her that even her husband hadn't seen. Andre had done more than look at that part, so shyness was thrown to the wind, along with caution.

"You want me to dress like a *putana* for you? Just remember," she pointed to the bedroom, "you'll have to keep me tied to your bed if you want me."

Andre stepped behind her. His wild, spicy scent filled her

head. She slipped her arms into the sheer fabric; he moved in front of her and pulled the robe closed around her waist. His gaze burned her.

The beginning of a smile lifted a corner of his mouth as he caressed her breast through the sheer fabric. "We shall see if I need to tie you again, my petite beauty." He held her hand while she stepped into the slippers.

"Oh, you're vile," she hissed and strode past him with her head held high.

"Wait!" he shouted.

Angela ignored him and walked into the bedroom. All signs of her humiliation gone. The oversized four-poster bed was made with a satin, pale-blue bedspread. With the navy-blue velvet drapes drawn wide, the Eiffel Tower, lit against the night sky, could be seen from the window.

Andre followed her. "This way, my dear," he said as he placed his gray jacket, warm from his body, over her shoulders and led her to a small table. He held out a high-back blue tufted chair shot with silver thread for her to sit. "This is James, my butler. He will see to our every need while we're here."

She felt heat rise into her cheeks. The butler must have seen her naked under the robe before Andre threw his jacket over her. James averted his eyes, but he must have heard. Then she thought, was he the one who removed the ties from the bed? Her gaze went back to the four-poster bed. Heat rose into her cheeks when she thought of what Andre had done to her on that bed. Her vagina pulsed.

"Champagne? We must toast to my good fortune in finding you at home, *ma belle*."

She held her tongue.

"What, my dear? You have no comment." He raised his glass to touch to hers. "Drink, *ma bell*." Andre never took his eyes from hers as he said, "James, that will be all. We can serve ourselves."

"Yes, sir." James bowed and left the room.

Once the door was closed, Angela stood, pushing back from the table, leaving his jacket where it laid on the chair. "You want to know what I think? You're a miserable son of a bitch... you're a bastard."

"Now, now, kitten, did you think I took care of myself?"

"I think you're a no good—"

"No." He shook his head. "No picking on my heritage. I know for a fact that my parents were married when I was born. Come sit down, or would you like to sit on my lap... Perhaps I should tie you to the chair?"

She sat so quickly, her bottom hurt, and his laughing did nothing to calm her.

"You surprise me, Angela. That face and that well-hidden body. I always knew you were a beauty. A classic Sicilian. Where did Giorgio get his aqua eyes from?"

She leaned forward and banged her fist on the table, sloshing the champagne in the crystal flutes. "Leave my son out of this. This is between you and me."

He reached across the tiny table set with china plates, taking a lock of her hair between his thumb and fingers, teasing it. "Your hair is drying with a nice curl. Another thing you have hidden in that old lady's bun you usually wear... I know it's your natural color."

She gazed into his silver eyes before she grasped how he knew. His gaze held a glint of mischief as she realized that he'd stripped her and, while she'd been blindfolded, he saw all of her. She pulled her hair from his hand. "Don't touch me."

"I'm going to do much more than touch." His black silk shirt spread open across his broad chest, showing her the smattering of his blond chest hairs. He must have shaved while she was in the bath. His aftershave drove her crazy with its spicy and sexy aroma. He lifted a broad shoulder in a shrug. "We have already, and that was only the beginning… an initiation of sorts. Eat. I don't want you to get drunk."

She hadn't eaten all day, but she didn't have an appetite. Angela didn't want to get drunk. She had to keep her wits about her and seize the moment to escape. Angela ate the lobster and steak that he put in front of her and drank little. She wasn't crazy about French food, drowning in butter, and didn't notice how delicious everything was.

Then he rang for his butler to take the meal away. Before the butler arrived, Andre said, "Let's go on the balcony." Taking her hand in his warm one, they walked out the French doors. The view of the Eiffel Tower, with its racing lights against the night sky, was magnificent. There was a chill in the December air. He'd brought out his jacket and draped it around her shoulders.

"Don't touch me," she snapped and pushed his jacket off, letting it fall to the stone floor. She wanted to jump on it, tread on it. Instead, she kicked his custom-made Armani jacket away from her feet.

Andre grabbed her to him. His big hands slipped to the curve of her buttocks, dragging her into his hard, unyielding body. He whispered, "Behave before I spank you like a naughty child."

She lifted her closed fists to his chest to shove at him. He held her tighter for a moment and then let her go. Andre picked up his jacket and once more wrapped it around her shoulders.

"Let's go in. It's too chilly out here for your stubborn nature."

"I'm not stubborn, you miserable man. Can't you see I don't want to be near you." She walked back to his bedroom.

"Come by the fireplace, my dear, so you don't catch a cold," he said from close behind her.

She willingly went to sit in one of the blue velvet wing chairs. Behind an ornate brass screen, the fire snapped and sizzled.

"That will be all, James. Bring breakfast up at the usual time." The butler silently closed the bedroom door as he left. Andre stood by the carved stone fireplace, an elbow on the black granite mantel. His shirt pulled tight across his bulging muscles. "You'll cover yourself in front of my staff."

Angela stood from the chair, bunched the jacket up, and flung it in his face. "You leave me to wear this flimsy garment, and then you tell me to cover myself—"

"What I give you to wear is for my pleasure, no others," he ground out.

"You don't know—"

He took a step toward her.

"No," she groaned and sat again.

Andre went to sit in the wing chair opposite her. She wouldn't look at him. Minutes, hours could have gone by before Angela lifted her head to see Andre stare into her eyes. The ice from earlier gone from the pewter depths, now she had a difficult time reading him.

"Come here," his husky voice whispered.

"No."

He sighed. "You'll learn to obey me."

"Obey? No, I certainly won't. What do you think I am, a child? You're nothing to me." She turned her head to stare into the fire. It made the room nice and toasty. It had been cold on the balcony, but she wouldn't give him the satisfaction of knowing that.

He broke into her thoughts. "I'm the man you made a deal with, the one who you owe a debt, for using me." His voice sounded like a clap of thunder.

"Didn't you do enough?" In one motion, he stood and pulled her up from the chair. He shoved the filmy garment from her shoulders, dragged it down her arms, and flung it across the room. It silently fluttered on to the Persian rug. Too late, she realized, all she did was antagonize him.

He was tall, so tall, she stood in the high-heel slippers and needed to stretch her neck to look into his silver eyes. She barely reached his shoulder.

Andre's lips set in a grim line before he gritted out, "Kneel."

She huffed at him, "I will not."

His big hands rested on her shoulders, the gradual pressure pushing her down.

"No," she hissed.

He pressed harder until her knees were on the plush carpet. She wouldn't look into his eyes, though when she focused directly in front of her, she saw the enormous bulge of his penis pressing against his black Armani pants. His thumb and forefinger held his waistband button, then he flicked his wrist and unbuttoned it. His hand came under her chin, lifting her until she gazed into his pewter eyes. "Unzip me," he said in a husky French accent.

She swallowed and shook her head.

"Do it."

Oh God. What was she going to do? *No tears, you can do this.* She raised her hands to his zipper. "I will always hate you for what you've done to me."

"Hate, love, it matters not."

She yanked on the zipper. "Easy, pussycat."

"Don't call—"

His voice was harsh. "I'll call you whatever I please." He caressed her cheek. "Now… be gentle."

Gentle? Her heart pounded as she slowly let the zipper down. She knew what he wanted, but dear God, she'd never, and he was so big. Even at rest, he was long and thick—

She took a breath and slid his pants down his long, muscular legs. It surprised her that he wore no underwear.

Andre stepped out of his pants. "What's wrong, pussycat?" He held his long shaft in one hand. The head was immense. Naked and kneeling at his feet, she glanced up at him and shook her head.

He touched her cheek, caressing her lips. The pad of his thumb lingered on her bottom lip, stroking back and forth. "Just like in the photo... Pussycat, take me in your hands, then—"

"So, that's what this is, a reenactment—"

"Do as I say," he firmly commanded.

Her heart skipped a beat. She shook her head. "No." Her voice broke out of her in a croak.

He stroked her cheek with the knuckles of his hand. Hesitantly, her fingers went around him. *He's so big.* She held his shaft at the base, marveling that his skin, so warm and smooth, covered a steel rod. He grew bigger. *Oh!* His scent, clean and sexy, filled her head.

"That's it, pussycat. Thinking of your mouth is making me harder. Hold me like that. *Bien.*" He held his shaft above her hand, and he rubbed the head of his massive erection against the seam of her lips.

It surprised her at how soft and smooth he was.

"Take me into your mouth."

Her heart hammered in her chest. Again, she shook her head. His hand came back to caress her cheek while he pressed the velvet soft head against her lips. She hesitated. He pressed forward, and she parted her lips. The tip of her tongue touched the swollen head.

"Ah," he groaned, "Yes, pussycat, use your tongue. Lick me."

She did as he ordered. Hesitantly, her tongue touched the head of his engorged penis. She wondered if she could do this. *I've done worse in my life.*

"That's it. Use your tongue. I know you're not shy, pussycat."

She pressed her tongue against his velvety smooth head and tasted a drop of moisture.

"Open your mouth."

She did, and he pushed into her to lie on her tongue.

"Use the tip of your tongue to press on the ridge under the head."

She did. "Ahh yes, pussycat."

She ran the tip of her tongue under and around. He cupped the back of her head with one large hand and flexed his lean hips, pushing an inch more into her mouth. She moved her tongue around the underside of his shaft.

"Open wider. Keep your teeth covered."

She did as he ordered. His hands held her head, his fingers clenched in her hair. She opened her mouth.

Andre pulled her head down. "Ah pussycat, your mouth was made for this," he said as he pushed more of himself in. "Look at me."

She raised her gaze to him.

"Keep your eyes open." He flexed his hips in short moves in and out of her mouth, then he said, "Ready."

Oh God, for what? His hard length filled her mouth. He moved in more and more. *Oh no.* He pushed down her throat. Her eyes rounded.

"Breathe through your nose… just a little more." She wrapped her fingers at the base of his shaft, pumping him. He curled his fingers over hers to teach her the motion. She tried to relax, taking more of his length into her mouth.

He groaned, "Good, pussycat." Then he held her head as he pulled out of her mouth and pushed in, not as deep. A few more short, quick strokes, and he filled her mouth again, going down her throat once more.

She reached her other hand up to hold his hip as he thrust in and out of her mouth, her tongue licking the underside.

"Yesss," he hissed. "Pussycat, let your tongue linger there... oh... yes, right there."

She didn't know what she was doing, but he was breathing faster, with his fingers tangled in her hair, holding her as he pumped in and out of her mouth.

Her pelvis felt heavy. She was wet, a sweet burn between her legs, and then her vagina pulsed. Her breasts ached, the nipples tight. Angela closed her eyes at the sensation.

"Open your eyes, look at me," he thundered.

Her lids were so heavy, she didn't know if she could.

"Open them," he hissed.

She did what he said, opening her eyes to gaze up at him as the tingling pulsations in her vagina took over, wave after wave of sheer pleasure.

Andre filled her mouth.

She moaned.

He smiled, looking at her. "Are you coming, pussycat? Your moan vibrated through me."

She couldn't answer. Andre pushed down her throat. Her body jerked with the shudders of her orgasm.

"My dick feels so good in your mouth, I can feel you coming... Soon, it will be my turn." Holding her hair wrapped in his hands, he pushed her head down on him as his hips came forward. He slipped deeper into her mouth. "You're going to swallow everything I have."

She remembered to breathe through her nose.

"Suck me. Yes, harder."

She did.

"Your mouth... ahh... ahh." He jerked forward, holding her head as he moved further down her throat—

Oh, oh. Angela's core pulsed, as a hot spurt of his seed shot into her mouth, then another and another. She had no choice but to swallow. He jerked again as she caressed his length with her mouth, sucking him as he'd said. When he finished, he stayed in her mouth for a moment, his breath heaving. He was glorious, his body covered in a sheen of perspiration, his muscles rippling. Angela looked into his silver eyes, then he slid from her mouth.

"Better than the photo… much better."

Her humiliation complete, she sat on her heels, head bent, mortified by her reaction to him.

"Get up and go lie on the bed." His voice was full of anger.

She jerked her head up, ready to curse him. All he did was lift a brow, and Angela held her head high and rose to her feet. She walked over to his bed. The covers were turned down at the foot. Angela lay on the edge.

"Scoot to the middle," he growled.

She did as she was told. *What is he up to?* She didn't know what he wanted.

His deep voice penetrated her thoughts. "Spread your legs."

She groaned, "Andre, please—"

"Do it," he thundered.

She did. *Why is he so angry? How many people has he used? It's only business.*

"More, wider, yes, that's it. Touch yourself."

"What?" She sat up. "I will not."

"Haven't you ever touched your pussy? Make yourself come?"

What was he talking about? She had closed herself off to physical contact of any kind. "I won't be turned into a slut for your benefit, to appease you for what you think I've done to you. Now let me go."

"You came while I was in your mouth. My pussycat has claws."

"Stop calling me that!" she shouted.

"Lie down, *ma belle*," he said in his husky French-accented voice.

She slowly lay back down, and he reclined on his side next to her. He crooked his elbow, and his head rested on his hand. He smiled at her. "Angela, spread your legs."

Her eyes closed. Then she moved her feet an inch apart.

"More, *ma belle*."

She shook her head.

"Shall I get the ties?" he asked in a whisper.

Angela spread her legs.

He laughed. "Good."

"You're a weak man," she bit out.

Andre's sculpted lips touched her breast, his hand at her abdomen. She felt his fingers spread over her belly. He opened his lips and drew her nipple deep into the inferno of his mouth, his hand slowly gliding over her. She was so hot for his touch with his mouth on her, he nibbled, and her nipple tightened. Her core was on fire. She held her hips still as he teased her breasts until she pushed her hips up, wanting him to touch her as he had before. "Andre," her voice was full of entreaty.

He released her nipple. "Touch yourself."

She groaned.

He took her hand and moved it to her mound. "Come on, I know you want to," he said. He pressed her fingers with his powerful hand. "Go ahead, pleasure yourself."

She turned her head away.

"No, pussycat, look at me. Move your fingers into that wet cunt."

She did what he said, and the zing of pleasure that shot through her surprised her.

He must have noticed because he said, "Yes, see how nice that feels? Use both hands, open yourself. I want to see your wet cunt."

She did.

"Now rub your clit. Back and forth." She did as he said and again, the delight tightened her pelvis, lifting her hips. Then she arched her back, her buttocks dug into the mattress.

"That's it. Rub your clit, it looks like a ripe berry ready to be—"

She couldn't hold back a moan of rapture.

"See how nice that feels? Shall I make you stop?"

She swallowed and shook her head, knowing that he could make her stop.

He laughed. "No? I think I'll help you. Your body is a delightful surprise."

She didn't understand, but her abdomen was so tight, she was alive with so many sensations.

Angela rubbed harder, her shallow breaths panted out of her, then she spread her thighs wider and lifted her knees, her feet planted on the mattress. Her clitoris was so sensitive, she was wild. She'd never done this to herself. And then he slid two of his fingers into her vagina. "I can't," she groaned.

"Yes, you can, *ma belle*. Whatever I want." Andre crooked his fingers.

Oh, the pleasure of that movement drove her so close to her orgasm, she dropped her hand from her sensitized clit.

"No, keep rubbing that beautiful berry, or I won't touch your G-spot again."

Was that what he was searching for? The pleasure pain was—he stroked that spot again and again until she was on fire. Her clitoris became the center of her universe. Her breath panted out of her. She was wound so tight and then in the next instant, she felt the clenching waves of her orgasm—

so powerful—she tried to pull his hand away. Her own hand fell away from her sensitized clit. Andre bent to suck her clit into his mouth. His tongue lashed at the tip, and another orgasm followed the first. Or was it one long one?

He stayed until the spasms slowed and finally stopped. She'd never felt anything as wonderful as what he made her do. She closed her eyes and fell asleep.

CHAPTER 4

$\mathcal{A}$ndre's gaze settled on Angela as she slept. She was a surprisingly sexy woman, feisty too. He touched his jaw. Her powerful punch stung. A smile tugged the corner of his lips. He knew that she never did much of the things he did to her and with her. He could tell that his dick was the first she'd ever taken into her sensuous mouth. His groin ached, thinking of that hot mouth and her lush lips around his shaft. She was a sexual creature, and she didn't even know it. The way she'd come when he touched her nipples, and then... the way she orgasmed while he was down her throat... Next time, he'd put a vibrator in her hot pussy while she sucked his dick. He wanted to feel her moans vibrate up his dick again.

Sleep eluded him as he lay in bed. He thought that his anger would have fled by now, but it lingered... He rose from the bed and went to pour himself a brandy. He sat in a blue velvet wing chair by the fireplace, watching her as she slept. She was a vixen, and he was going to enjoy using her.

To manipulate him with her devious plan. He ground his

teeth before he let out a long breath. Andre couldn't believe the audacity, no… the balls she had. The way she'd arranged for him to meet Ricardo and Liz. The way she'd asked him in her sweet voice to buy stocks in the Contessa cruise line of DiMarco Enterprises and then her devious plan to use him in her takeover bid. Between the shares she owned and what she asked him to buy… how many other shareholders had she manipulated?

Andre rose from his chair by the fireplace and crawled back into bed with his new play toy. He slid close to her and put an arm over the curve of her delicate waist, holding her near. In her sleep, she snuggled her back against him, and her woman's scent filled his head. He fell asleep thinking of her seductive curves and not her manipulative nature.

Andre awoke, staring at the ceiling. Then he heard a sound… where… she wasn't in the bed. He heard the noise again, following the sound into his study. Angela was in the white robe that covered nothing, bent over his laptop. Her curly black hair fell over half her face as it reached past her shoulders. She hit at the keys, cursing in Italian.

"Trying to contact someone?"

She jumped back. "Where did you put my clothes? I'm finished with you, you *bastardo*."

"Oh, no, you're finished when I say you are… Clothes are only what I allow you to wear. For now… back on the bed… face down… I think."

"No. Haven't you done enough? I won't allow you to punish me with your filthy… dirty perversions for what you believe I did to you. Poor, poor you."

Andre was at her side in two strides, grabbed the robe and, as before, yanked it from her lethal body, throwing it to the floor. He kept the satin tie in his hand and bent to lift her over his shoulder. He strode to the bedroom.

"Put me down now," she shrieked, beating at his naked back with her fists.

He whacked her bottom, not hard, but enough to get her attention.

"Oh, you're a beast. Put me down."

"Okay, wildcat." He threw her onto the bed.

She scrambled to get up, pushing her jet-black hair from her face. Angela swung her closed fist at him. This time, he was prepared. Reaching for her wrist, he pulled her arm behind her back. She yanked a fistful of his hair with her other hand. Andre grabbed that wrist and pinned her down on the bed with his body.

"Get off. Get off me," she yelled, trying to buck him from her.

He smiled, piercing her eyes. "Wildcat, I'm going to make you beg me to never get off you."

"No, I won't," she ground out between gritted teeth.

He shifted his weight off her and rolled her onto her stomach.

"Oh, stop." She yanked her arm.

He held her down, dragging her arms up over her head as he tied her wrists together. Then he tied the satin belt to the center slat of the headboard. She lay on her stomach, and her derriere rose as she yanked on her wrists. He couldn't resist caressing the firm satin globes of her buttocks.

"Don't touch me," she yelled.

"Crawl up onto your knees." His hand lingered on her buttock.

"*Bastardo.* No, you filthy bastard."

He laughed. "I think I'll have to gag you again. My name is Andre, and I'll remind you once more that my parentage is not in doubt."

"You're a piece—" The gag was back in her mouth, and he

knotted the fabric behind her head. "Much better. Now on your knees."

"Mmm agghh."

"Oh no, you don't want to." More grunts from around her gag. He straddled her as she tried to buck him off. His lips moved to her neck. "Oh, wildcat, you will do as I say." He ran his hands down her spine to the curve of her buttocks.

She struggled against his weight as well as the satin ties on her wrists. He would make her beg. He would drive her mad with wanting him. Andre sat back on her thighs and massaged the firm, silky flesh of her buttocks with both hands. He rubbed and kneaded the twin globes.

She tried to buck him off, but he held her smooth, satin butt under his hands. His fingers digging into the firm flesh massaging her, he said, "Your body was made for this. I'm going to fuck you any way I want." He separated her cheeks and stroked down between the firm flesh. Andre couldn't help himself. He leaned over and spread kisses over her spine and around her buttocks, dragging his tongue down the center.

She screamed into the gag. Angela squirmed and yelled. He nudged one of his knees between her legs and then his other, pushing his knees apart to spread her thighs. She tried to wiggle away from his touch. Andre nipped her buttocks while his finger stroked between her legs. He separated her black curls, and his finger found her clitoris, rubbing at it, ignoring her shrieks and screams into the gag. He kneeled between her thighs. "Your cunt is wet, but I can make you wetter." He rubbed her clit. "Rise up on your knees."

She shook her head, yelling into the gag.

"Not yet?"

In this position, she was open to him, and he rubbed at her clit. He thrust his middle finger into her center, slow strokes in and out, coaxing her to wet his finger. He didn't ignore her clit, moving back to press on the bud. It was big and ripe for him. He rolled that delicate piece of flesh between his finger and thumb.

Angela lifted her buttocks. She wasn't objecting now. A smile broke across his lips. She rose her buttocks up, opening herself to his sexual massage.

"You like that?"

"Mmm, grr." She shook her head.

He could feel her quiver over his finger. Her thighs shook, and still she fought him. He thrust a second finger into her. She pushed up.

"Oh, pussycat, on your knees." He would make her do whatever he wanted. The way she had manipulated him ate at his gut, and he would humble her before he was satisfied.

ANGELA LAY ON HER STOMACH, while Andre forced her body to respond. She was on fire. The throb in her took her breath away. His fingers rubbed at her. *Oh God, so good.* And then, thrusting into her from this angle, he was relentless, and she couldn't control herself. Her knees moved on the mattress. Her hands clasped almost in a plea, with her wrists tied together and the sash tied to the headboard. Lying face down, her breasts dug into the mattress, and she couldn't stop her buttocks from rising, opening herself to his wishes. He stretched her thighs wider apart with his knees. Now she moved to catch his fingers, wanting more than the featherlight touch he teased her with. Needing more pressure, *there, there. Oh, he is missing the....*

His husky voice broke in, "Rise higher on your knees, *ma belle.*"

She fought the urge to do as he said. He slowed his touch on her clitoris. Her own body fought with her as she moved her knees up the mattress. She was open to him, not caring, only needing to feel the burning pleasure he gave her.

O Dio, santo cielo. Andre pressed on her clitoris, and bursts of fiery sensations raced through her body. Needing him in her, she lifted her buttocks and spread her knees wider.

"Wildcat, now you'll be rewarded." His sexy voice held the promise of his words.

She waited for the thrust of his penis, but what he did… *oh, oh. Ah,* she felt the lash of his tongue on her clit. Flames of fire erupted in her as he licked her in this position. She couldn't think, only feel what he did. Then he sucked her clit into his mouth, and all she wanted was to push back on his mouth and that magic tongue, so he could make her climax.

He was so strong, a mass of muscles. He lifted her, exposing her wet sex to his mouth, with his tongue thrusting faster and deeper, bringing her close to orgasm.

He stopped, and she whimpered into the gag, *Oh God, don't leave me like this.*

Andre rolled over onto his back. He held her hips so that she pressed down on him. She almost screamed. Her ties were long enough that she could move, and he forced her to rise onto her knees. He lay on his back, his head between her spread thighs, and held her to his mouth. His tongue, oh, his tongue going into her vagina from this angle, and his lips sucking on her clitoris. His fingers dug into her hips, holding her so he could lick and suck all of her. Andre's big hands shifted her hips back and forth, moving her over his mouth, his tongue going into her vagina.

The moan came from deep in her throat as she lost all inhibition and moved on him. Her body took charge. She gyrated wildly on his mouth, needing his tongue to go deeper into her. Her orgasm came in a gush of scandalous pleasure, so unbelievably lustful.

She fell forward, heart racing as if she ran up twelve flights of stairs.

Andre untied her wrists, turning her over as he said, "The gag stays if you can't control your cursing."

She reached for the piece of fabric and pulled it off. "Oh… you."

His blond-cropped hair mussed, and his pewter eyes held a hint of silver. They were shining with mischief. "No, no." He wagged his finger at her. "Now make nice. We aren't finished." He bent to take a breast in his hand, the nipple already a hard bud needing his mouth to soothe it. She didn't have a chance to move. He spread her legs. His erection teased at her entrance and pushed into her heat. "Nice and wet for me." He lifted her. "Wrap your legs around me."

Her head tipped back, and she lifted her legs, holding his massive biceps in her hands. Andre thrust in, pulled almost completely out, thrust deeper, out, in deeper, deeper. She stretched to hold him in her sheath, the friction of his pumping into her faster and faster as he drove her. Angela's toes curled. She was wild as another orgasm had her shuddering around him, holding his huge maleness into her as her inner muscles stroked his length.

"Wildcat, a little more, yes."

She lifted her legs higher on his waist, taking him deeper into her, coaxing him toward his climax. He thrust, and they came together in jolting waves of bliss. He pushed her hair back from her damp brow and kissed her temple. She lay content in his arms.

"Now be a good girl and go to sleep."

"Oh, you filthy—"

"Do I have to tie you to my bed?"

She realized he was purposefully provoking her, but she

wouldn't let him. She lay there. "No, you don't need to." *I would never tell you, but I love everything you do to me.*

"*Bien.*" He wrapped his arms around her, snuggling against her back as he tucked his knees under hers. She listened to his even breathing as they both fell asleep.

ANDRE PEERED at Angela from under his fringe of lashes. He'd kept her up most of the night, making love, and she'd slept into the late afternoon. When she woke up, she said, "I know I was wearing a dress when you drugged me. Did you take me naked from my home?"

He rose from the wing chair by the fire and walked over to her. "I like you nude or in the robe—easy access."

"You're a pig." She swung her legs from the bed and stood.

He handed her the sheer garment.

She balled it up and threw it in his face.

"Naked it is. I'll bring lunch up for you. Then I must go out for a time."

"You're leaving me here?"

"Yes, I have to lock the door from the outside, because I can't trust you—"

"Are we trying for civility? You don't even know how." She turned her back to him.

He ran his hand over her naked backside and whispered into her ear, "When I return, we can explore my civility." His fingers lingered on a rounded, firm globe before he gently squeezed.

"Get away from me." She spun around and shoved him.

He shook his head. *She's a fiery temptress.* "I'll be back with lunch."

He came back with her food on a tray and placed it on a table by the fireplace. She sauntered over to it, lifted the china plate, and then turned the contents over into the fireplace. Her temper excited him. "Not hungry? I see you didn't dump the wine. Don't get drunk."

"*Bastardo.*" She cursed at him.

He'd be prepared at dinner. Andre locked the bedroom door from the outside. When he returned, he found her sleeping on the bed. She was beautiful. Curves in all the right places, her big, high breasts, were such a surprise. Her fit body and that tight pussy. How could she be such a contradiction?

He woke her. "You won't deny yourself nourishment. Let's eat in the study so Danielle can clean the mess you made." He led the way to a table set for them. "My chef went out of his way to prepare a nice seafood risotto for you. I have a wonderful bottle of wine to go with it… Perhaps you've heard of… Lombardo Wines."

Her head snapped up, eyes flaring and shooting darts of fire at him. "I don't care, and I'm not hungry."

"Sit with me, m*a belle.*" He pulled out a chair for her.

She crossed her arms and tapped her bare foot. "No."

"Oh, perhaps you'd like to sit on my lap, and I could feed you."

"Don't touch me."

"Please sit, *ma belle.*" He held out the chair, and she swept her sheer robe as if it were a ball gown and slid onto the seat. The sheer fabric accented every part of her magnificent backside; the rounded cheeks of her buttocks beckoned his hand as she sat. He moved to his chair. *Let her eat and then…*

He could see the way she pretended not to be upset, but all he had to do was remind her he could easily tie her up again. It was only a threat. He liked her spunk. He rubbed his jaw, remembering the punch she had thrown at him. Andre hid the smile. He figured he deserved her punch and more. She ate the risotto without any comment. When he poured the wine, she said, "You are a mean-spirited man, to choose a wine from my son's label."

His gaze held hers, then a smile tugged at his lips. He lifted his wineglass and sipped the delicate white wine. The flavor lingered on his tongue. "I thought you would like it. Giorgio sent me a case of this and a case of red last year." They ate the rest of the meal in silence. He rang for James to remove the meal.

"Let's go before they come in." Andre took Angela into the sitting room and closed the door behind them.

"Come, pussycat, sit with me."

She turned to him, her hands on her hips. "How long will you keep me here?"

He sat on the sofa. "Hmmm," he leaned back. "Until I feel avenged. We had a bargain."

"Avenged? Grow up," she sneered. "I did nothing you didn't want me to do. You were happy to help buy stocks for me—I might add—with my own money. You were more than happy to fuck someone who you thought was Ricardo's girlfriend."

He gazed at her, mocking her. "Your language—"

"Yes? What about my language?" She moved her hands from her hips. "I don't like what you say and what you call me."

"Really? What do you want me to call you, pussycat?"

"You make it sound like a slur... I loathe the day my son met you. You're mean and vindictive. When I think about how I believed you. That you would help me—"

"Oh, don't make yourself out to be the wronged party, so pure and innocent. You tried to steal Ricardo's cruise ship company. You were so sweet when you asked for my help to buy stocks for you. You went so far as to offer yourself as the prize; we made a deal that day. What happened, did you think I wouldn't accept?"

"There is no deal. What have you done with the stocks? The shareholders meeting is next month. I want Ricardo to suffer. My son Giorgio should have been the CEO and not my nephew."

"I sold them back to Ricardo, and dear sweet pussycat… I'm keeping the money. You have used me from the beginning."

"Oh, you bastard."

He ignored her outburst. "I want to know why you are so adamant about this. Your son is happy as president of Lombardo Wines. Isn't he the chairman of the board of DiMarco Enterprises?"

She turned away from him and crossed her arms.

He patted the sofa cushion beside him. "Come sit down and tell me, *ma belle*, why did you… close yourself off after your husband died? All these years later, you continue to mourn him."

"Don't talk about my husband." She bowed her head before she whispered, "A tragic loss for me."

Giorgio had said that his father died in a car accident when he was nine. Andre watched Angela swat at a tear. Her throat muscles moved as she tried to compose herself. Andre didn't want to push her, then he heard her whisper, "We'd argued that morning about… something… that now is so stupid."

"Angela, it is none of my business, but all these years…"

"His mother meddled in our personal business. Things that concerned only a husband and wife. Sal said he wanted to go for a drive, to clear his head, think about everything. He'd said he didn't want to lose me, and that's the day I lost him." Angela took a deep breath and let it out slowly. "Fortunately for him, he didn't suffer long. He left the suffering to me. And the guilt, I blame myself for pushing Sal… but that didn't prevent me from turning my anger on his mother…

the doctors said there wasn't anything they could do. It was a matter of time, but I wouldn't let her see him in the hospital. I sat by his side, holding his hand until… there wasn't any more life in his body." Angela wrapped her arms around herself.

"I was young when we married. I was determined to marry him, even though my parents felt he was too old for me. He was ten years older but when you have just turned fifteen, twenty-five is old. We got married anyway, and I got pregnant right away with Giorgio. Sal and my brother started DiMarco Enterprises together. My husband was happy, and so was I. Salvatore loved making wine, and he had a great vineyard where we lived. Then… in the blink of an eye, it was over. I hated living there without him. I hated his mother. It made no sense. I hated everyone, including my brother and his family. I don't know why, but I lashed out at everyone.

When my husband died, I was twenty-four with a nine-year-old son. Being a woman, I couldn't take on a corporate position—my brother took Giorgio under his wing, promising me that Giorgio would always be a part of the corporation. I watched as my son was pushed to the side, while Ricardo was groomed to become CEO."

Andre had never heard Angela talk so much about her family and her husband. Her voice was full of sorrow.

He wanted to console her. "People leave, they don't mean to it happens. I know my wife didn't want to die. We were happy planning a family, and then it was over."

Angela lifted her head and gazed into his eyes. "You… were married? I… never knew."

"Yes, for almost two years. Her name was Adrianna. She loved Paris."

"How? I mean, what happened?" He strained to hear her voice.

The slight movement of her fingers as she almost reached for his hand was not lost on Andre. "It's not about me, Angela. So, is that why you tried to destroy your nephew?"

She bent her head, gripped her hands in her lap, and wouldn't look at him.

"Yes, I hated watching my nephew in his glorious penthouse with all his women gracing the covers of magazines, while my son toiled in Palermo—"

Andre's brows came together. "Toiled? Angela, I know your son and believe me, he does not toil. He does what he wants and what he enjoys. He has his own jet and travels to his many vineyards. And his position as chairman on the board of DiMarco Enterprises keeps him busy."

The lights on the Eiffel Tower went out. "It's one in the morning. Let's go to bed." He was as hard as granite.

"Where?"

"In my bed, of course."

"No."

"Yes."

"I won't lie in the same bed with you."

"You did last night, and now you will; first to make love and then to sleep."

"Why do you insist on calling it love?"

"Okay, I'm easy. First to fuck and then to sleep." He stood from the lush, cream-colored sofa and locked his fingers around her delicate wrist, pulling her up.

"No, I won't."

"We will see." He stopped, and his brows came together. "Are you sore?"

"I'm not telling you anything. Get away." She yanked her arm, and then her head came up.

"Yes," she sighed. "I'm… sore… yes, very sore."

He smiled at her, seeing right through her ploy. "Ok no fu—sex. We will just rest together." He rubbed his jaw with his other hand. "Yesterday—Your right hook is pretty powerful. Kiss my cheek and make it better."

"No, I'm not kissing anything."

"We will see." He separated her robe, looking at her breasts. "I'm sorry if I was rough with you yesterday. I don't see any bruises though. Do your breasts hurt?"

She stamped her foot. "I told you. I'm... No... nothing hurts."

"Good, come lie with me."

"Andre, this is crazy. I'm so much... older than you... It's quite insane."

"No, it isn't. Will you tell me why?"

"Why what? I don't want to talk about anything. How long will you keep me here?"

"Indefinitely fucking you, however and wherever I want, as often as I want."

"At some point, my family will look for me... my son—"

"He thinks you have taken an extended vacation."

"What? How?"

"I texted him from your phone. Now it's turned off and nowhere that you can get at it."

"Oh, you're definitely low, a bastard. I—"

"Again, I thought we cleared up that issue."

"You're a mean and vulgar man... one who is easily insulted... thin skinned. That's what you are. You think I don't know what a piece of—" She sputtered to a stop.

Andre grabbed her shoulders, a leer on his face. He reached for his pants zipper—

Her eyes rounded, and she shook her head. "No, I... I... won't."

"Yes, you will. When you take me into your lying mouth, then you can't talk. I want you to bathe me with your tongue."

She moaned. "Aww, I—"

"On your knees."

"No, I won't."

"Shall I tie you?" He unbuttoned his white silk shirt.

She shook her head. "Just remember that I'll always hate you."

"I remember your eagerness for me to buy the stocks… your sweet promise of days and nights in my arms." He pulled his zipper down and stepped out of his pants.

"Agghh, you're a mean man to hold me to that bargain," she said, kneeling at his feet.

"Remove your robe and give me the tie."

She slipped the robe off her shoulders and down her arms to fall in a puddle around her lethal curves. Her hand trembled as she handed over the satin belt.

"I just want to move your hair from your face, *ma belle.*" He smoothed the mass of thick, silky curls from her face and tied the satin belt to hold her hair back. "Better?"

She swallowed and looked up at him.

"Your mouth is beautiful; your lips are full and swollen." He ran the pad of his thumb along her bottom lip, pressing and rubbing. Looking into her eyes, he said, "Hold me in your hand and bathe my dick with your tongue."

Her cheeks pinked, and her long black lashes rested on the delicate flush as she closed her eyes.

"No, *ma belle,* keep your eyes open. Look at me."

Angela moved forward, her small hand extended, and her fingers curled around the base of his throbbing cock. She lowered her mouth. He held back a groan as her little pink tongue licked his length; it felt like satin against his skin. The tip of her tongue traced a blue vein up the side of his dick, then she lashed at the ridge of sensitive skin on the underside of his swollen head.

"Oh, pussycat, you have learned some tricks."

She swirled her tongue around him, again finding his

trigger with the tip of her sweet tongue. *Oh God, I'm going to explode.*

"Take me in your mouth." His voice sounded strange to him, as a groan came from deep in his chest.

She took him into the warm cavern of her mouth and sucked.

"Awwhhaa, yes," the words shot out of him. Andre sank his fingers into her jet-black hair, holding her sweet mouth on him. His hips jerked forward, and he moved down her throat. He gazed at her as she sucked him. Her hand moved to cup his balls. Every muscle tensed as he gritted his teeth. The sweet suction of her mouth, her warm open palm on him, drove him like a locomotive to climax. He came in a furious rush, and she swallowed his bursts of come. She licked every drop from him. No woman but her had ever been so perfect. She stayed on her knees, sitting on her heels. Her head bent.

He removed the tie and then reached his hand under her chin and lifted her head. Andre looked deeply into her eyes as desire blazed from her black gaze. "*Ma belle.*" He caressed the delicate olive skin of her cheek with his thumb before he lifted her and sat on the sofa, dragging her onto his lap. Her back was to his chest, as he held an arm around her waist. Her head dipped to his shoulder, his forearm pushed her breasts up, and his fingers played with a nipple.

"You came," she groaned.

He squeezed a nipple between his thumb and finger.

"Ahh," she moaned against his throat.

"Spread your legs, pussycat."

She did.

"Wider," he said and separated his knees, pushing her thighs further apart. She lay sprawled across him, her big breasts pushed up by his forearm, her nipples pointed and ripe for him. "Let's see how wet you are." His finger sank into her. "Oh, yes, very wet." His long finger traced up her folds and reached her clit. "So nice and big, a hidden pearl needing my attention. Do you like when I suck your clit into my mouth?"

She groaned, "Yes."

He rubbed and circled her bud. "So nice, Angela," he said as he slid his finger into her vagina.

CHAPTER 5

*H*e nibbled on her earlobe before he said, "Touch your breasts for me. Let me see you pull on your nipples."

"No."

He used his thumb and forefinger to press on her clit.

"Oh," she gasped, writhing against him.

"You like that, I can tell. Now do that to your nipples."

"Oh, please," she groaned, her head pressing on his shoulder. She was beautiful draped over his body.

He ran his lips along the delicate skin behind her ear. Her scent, orange blossom and sex, filled him. He kissed the side of her neck, sucking the satin skin into his mouth, needing to mark her. "Here, like this," he whispered in her ear as his other hand moved on her breast. He took an excited nipple between his thumb and finger and pulled at the same time his other hand pulled on her clitoris.

"*Dio. Ahhh, ahhh, santo cielo.*" She shivered in his arms, opening her legs over his thighs.

"See how nice that feels. You do that, and then I can use my fingers to fuck your pussy."

Angela groaned, squirming on his lap, her hair spilled over his shoulder. He swelled hard again, and her buttocks pressed on his erection.

"Oh, Andre."

"Yes, my dick wants more."

Her head rolled on his shoulder, as she moved her hand to her breast.

"Both hands," he whispered, kissing the delicate skin behind her ear once more before he ran his tongue along the curve of her neck.

Taking her nipples with trembling fingers, Angela's breath hissed out of her.

He lifted her lethal body to hold her on him, and then he thrust two fingers into her wet pussy. "You're so hot, you're dripping all over my fingers."

She stopped.

"Keep playing with your nipples."

She lifted her hands and did as he said. He rubbed her clit, as Angela arched against his chest, and he thrust two fingers into her, finding her G-spot. She moaned and squirmed on his lap, while he kissed her neck and spread his knees wider to hold her in place. He reached deeper into her wet pussy, dragging the pads of his fingers over her sensitive skin.

Her breath came in shallow gasps as she arched against him. "Andre, *santo cielo*. Holy heaven above." She screamed, and her body shuddered in orgasm. Her hands fell away from her breasts, but he kept his thumb on her clit and his fingers curling on her G-spot. He could feel the pulsing clenches of her climax. He kept his fingers deep in her, not moving until the last shudder left her body.

Then he slid his fingers in deeper, forcing another orgasm from her petite body. "You like the way my fingers fuck you? You're quivering on the verge of another orgasm." He stroked her G-spot.

She panted against his neck. Her glorious big breasts rising and falling with each breath, and then her head rolled on his shoulder.

"Oh, ahh… Andre," His name was a whisper on her lips

Sprawled across his body in all her naked glory, Angela turned her head. He gazed into her black eyes. They were clouded with a sexual haze before she slid her lids down over them. The fringe of her dark lashes laid on her flushed cheeks. She looked vulnerable, and his fingers stopped. Her finely arched brows drew together in confusion.

Andre couldn't help himself. He dipped his head and brushed his lips over her plump pink ones, lingering at the corner before his mouth covered hers. He wanted to memorize the texture of her sweet lips with his. She trembled in his arms. He held back a groan and with gentle sweeps across her swollen lips, he held her to him. She opened to his demands, and his tongue explored the recesses of her mouth. Her taste intoxicated him… Andre hadn't felt this way—not in a long time, maybe never. He held her willing body; she turned in his arms, clinging to him while he kissed her with an overwhelming hunger. She kissed him back, sliding her tongue along his. Her surrender drove him, never feeling anything so all-consuming as a willing Angela.

Her kisses were the sweetest thing he had ever tasted. He sucked her tongue into his mouth, while her fingers danced in his hair, moving to the nape of his neck. She slanted her hot mouth over his, their tongues entwined, and her passion drove him on. He memorized the texture of her, knowing he would always crave this seductress as no other. Her other hand furrowed into his chest hair, caressing him. Her sweet mouth was made for kissing—

He stopped as his brain caught up to his emotions. What am I doing, kissing her? He tore his mouth from hers. Her eyes opened, rounding in surprise, and he shoved her from his lap. "On your knees." He thundered, consumed with rage.

She caught herself from stumbling and stood before him in all her naked glory, her hair a mass of tiny ringlets cascading around her. Her nipples were pink and extended, her black-as-night eyes blazing. "I hate you." She wiped her swollen lips with the back of her hand.

He didn't miss the innuendo of that move. "Good, I want your hate, but it will never match mine for you. Now get down on all fours."

She didn't move. "You will have to make me."

He rose from the sofa, almost knocking her over in his fury. "Oh, I'll make you do whatever I wish." He reached for her shoulders. "Kneel."

She lifted her chin, the defiance plainly showing in her stance and in her blazing eyes.

He applied pressure to her shoulders. "You'll bend to my will."

The fury in her black gaze excited him as he pressed his erection against her stomach. She groaned and fought his hands, first grabbing at them, and then she swung her closed fist at the center of his chest. He ignored the pain of her punch and applied just enough pressure so she had no choice but to do what he wanted. She knelt before him. He held his erection. "See what you do to me. I want you again."

He rubbed the head of his swollen penis against her cheek and her lips. "Get on all fours." *Tell me you don't want this.*

She flashed her anger at him. Andre ignored that and pressed his dick to her mouth. Her lips compressed before she moved so she was on her hands and knees. He stepped to stand behind her.

"Spread your knees wider, wildcat." He knelt behind her. His swollen dick throbbed to be in her hot pussy, needing to take her. "Lower your arms and rest your head on your forearms. Lift your cunt to me, pussycat. Yes, just like that."

"I do hate you. You have a thin skin to be so put off by what I did, using you for my gain. Poor, poor you."

"Shut up." He held her hips. "Spread your knees wider."

She didn't move. He ground his teeth. Somewhere in the back of his mind, he admired her defiance. How she wouldn't bend to his will, he squashed that thought. He caressed her buttocks with one hand. Caressing her inner thigh, he moved his hand forward and cupped her mound. He touched her clit. She gasped and arched her back, lifting her buttocks, opening herself to him. He kept his finger on her clit, adding pressure as the pad of his finger rested on the bud.

She moaned and slid back, rubbing her clit on his finger.

"Spread your knees... Pussycat." Andre knew she hated being called that.

She spread them, and he positioned his throbbing erection at the entrance to all that hot, wet heat. She tried to move back and take him into her body. He held her hips still. With one hand, he pressed his erection over her wet folds, rubbing her. She moaned and tried to take him into her body. He ran his hand up her spine to her shoulders, then back to hold her hips and pushed the head of his penis into her heat.

"Mmm, ahh, yes," she moaned, and her body trembled.

"Let me hear what you want."

She shook her head, her jet-black hair a mass of curls spread out over her forearms and on the Persian rug.

"No? Let's see, pussycat." He reached his finger around and rubbed her clit with a small amount of pressure. A smile tugged at his lips when she tried to move on his finger. "Not until you tell me what you want."

Again, she shook her head. Andre rubbed her clit, adding more pressure. He felt her body coil and knew she couldn't take too much more before she came. He prevented her from moving, taking him into her hot cunt as he rubbed and shifted his hips to push his dick in an inch.

"Ahh… ahh, yes," she moaned louder. He shifted his hips back, taking away the little bit of his cock he'd given her.

"Tell me. I want you to say fuck my pussy." *You won't ever wipe my kiss from your lips again.* He pressed forward.

"Agh," she groaned, panting large puffs of air.

He started to pull out.

"Please… Andre, please," she groaned.

He didn't move. She kept her head on her forearms but turned to look up at him, her obsidian gaze blazing at him.

"I hate you," she yelled.

He nudged forward, giving her more of his cock, while his finger slipped over her clit, rubbing back and forth. Her body trembled. He stopped moving, the head of his cock in her wet cunt. He had to get back in control. "Your clit feels so nice, big, and slick with your need." He teased her flesh between his thumb and forefinger.

She lifted her buttocks, whimpering, "fu… fuck my pussy," she said in a breathy whisper.

"Did you say something? I couldn't hear you."

She pounded her fist on the floor. "Ohhh. Fuck. My. Pussy."

He rubbed her clit once more before he held her hips in his hands. "Yes, much better." He thrust forward and in one swift move, he buried himself to the hilt in her wet, hot cunt. Savoring the pleasure of her tight heat as his dick throbbed. She was more than any other woman had ever been. Her anger, her erotic pleasure—

"Ohhh, ahh." She screamed and came in waves of hot pulses, holding him in her.

When her shudders stopped, he said, "You won't provoke me, Angela. I'm going to use you at my leisure for as long as I deem fit." He gripped her satin-smooth hips. Lifting her buttocks, he pulled out of her tight pussy, keeping only his throbbing head in. Then he thrust into her again. "Ahhh," he groaned and pulled almost fully out. He slammed into her again and again.

Angela was just as excited and pushed back as he moved forward, allowing him to go deeper. "Ahh, O Dio mio." She clutched him in her as another orgasm began.

"That's it. Stroke me into you, hold me in your hot pussy." His fingers curled around her hips, and he ground into her. "Feel my balls against your wet cunt."

She was coming, and he continued to pump and thrust into her, pushing her to another climax. Gritting his teeth, he fought his own release. Struggling to hold on, he exploded into her. He poured his seed into Angela's tight, hot pussy, amazed that he could come again. He stayed in her, letting her milk him.

Andre collapsed forward, keeping his weight on his arms. He kissed her back, between her shoulder blades. When her shudders stopped, he pulled out. He stood and helped her from the floor. "Get on the bed."

She stood tall, gazed into his eyes, and gave a slight shake of her head.

"My Sicilian goddess is always defiant. Do it now."

Angela walked to the bed with all the dignity she could muster, being naked and having begged him for the pleasure he gave her in yet another position she'd never made love in.

"Lie on the bed," he said.

A zing of excited desire coursed through her, and she knew she would. She gazed at him as he walked naked to the bar. He took two cut crystal glasses from the shelf and then poured whiskey into them. She couldn't help admiring his lean, masculine beauty. Extremely tall, his blond hair tousled, those broad shoulders and narrow hips. His arms were massive like the rest of him, and he was covered in a sheen of sweat. Not an ounce of fat, lean muscle shifted and rippled over his sculpted body.

He'd just come, and his glorious cock was still hard. Angela couldn't take her eyes off his erection and the springy, blond hair between his muscular legs. She couldn't believe she was able to get him in her mouth. She fought the urge to touch her lips; they felt puffy.

"Here, drink. It will help you relax." He handed her the glass and leaned against the headboard, stretching his legs out in front of him, and tipped the crystal glass to his lips. He drank half his drink in one shot. She sipped at hers, enjoying the warmth of the smooth liquor. When he finished his drink, she handed him her glass, and he placed them both on the nightstand.

"Go to sleep," he said.

Angela clenched her teeth, and then she stopped. "Can I have a cover?"

He looked at her. "Are you cold?"

Dio, he makes me so hot. "No."

"Then lie down and go to sleep," he murmured.

Her anger rose. "I'm not a child," she sneered at him.

He grinned, and his eyes traveled over her naked body. "Oh, do I know you're not." He tugged her to him. "If you don't want to sleep… we can…" His silky voice held a challenge

Angela moved out of his arms and laid her head on the pillow, closing her eyes. His deep-bellied laugh filled the room. Her eyes snapped open, and she ground her teeth. "You're a mean and thin-skinned man to treat me so."

He rolled onto his side and trailed his fingers along her belly. "I know, *ma belle.*"

Angela wouldn't let him goad her. She wanted to scratch

his eyes out. She shoved his hand away from her and closed her eyes.

She must have fallen asleep because the next thing she knew, he was covering her with a satin down-filled comforter. Bright sunlight filled the bedroom. She closed her eyes again.

Andre spoke in French, "You may enter, Joseph."

"Good morning, sir. Breakfast as you requested."

"Put it on the table, and then you may go."

"Yes, sir."

Since she'd walked in front of the butler in the see-through robe, Andre made sure that she was always covered, or in another room when Joseph was around. She had been mortified when she'd done that, but she was angrier at Andre.

"I know you're awake. Let's eat. I'm famished." He slipped the blanket from her body.

"I'm not hungry."

He reached to pull her into his arms; she jumped out of the bed and grabbed the flimsy robe to wrap around herself. He laughed.

"You think it's funny that I would rather eat this lousy excuse for food you feed me than have your perverted filthy hands on my body."

"After breakfast, we'll see if you can beg me not to touch you."

"*Si un uomo senza—*"

"Tsk, tsk, pussycat. No cursing in Italian."

She couldn't understand this new anger and the way he provoked her, calling her pussycat with that sneer in his voice. Since he'd kissed her, he seemed to do everything he could to bring her down a peg. To have her at his mercy. To beg him and then, oh, she'd been mortified by her total submission to his erotic sex.

Angela sat opposite him. He poured her coffee and handed her a plate with a pastry. She bit into the sweet confection and ate with a hunger she didn't realize she had. The pastries were okay, a little too full of custard for the morning. She preferred a croissant with some jam. The espresso was good, nice, and strong the way she liked it. She poured a second cup as she watched Andre through the fringe of her lashes. *He is a very handsome man. His hair cropped short in the latest style, so nice, his jaw covered in morning stubble. How would that feel against my—What am I saying?*

Andre had put on a pair of gray lounge pants. She bristled that he kept her in the sheer robe. Angela placed her empty cup on the table. Confused by her thoughts, she tried to hide her discomfort.

"Let's take a shower so I can wash my filthy hands."

She saw the set of his jaw and knew he was angry, but she didn't care. "I hate you."

"I know, pussycat. Especially when you scream in pleasure."

He rose from his seat, and she said, "I will not—"

He lifted her out of her chair and carried her over his shoulder. When his big hand stroked her buttock, Angela kicked her legs and beat her fists at his back. He walked into his bathing chamber and stood her on her feet.

She moved away from him.

Andre turned the gold-tone knob, and all six shower-heads came on at once. With one hand, he untied the slip knot on his lounge pants and dropped them to the floor. Before she knew what he was doing, he'd slid her robe off her shoulders and pulled her into the marble and glass-enclosed shower. "Andre—"

"Yes, *ma belle*. You're beautiful. I love your classic Sicilian beauty. He took a bar of soap and made a lather with his hands. She stood still, staring at him. *He thinks I'm beautiful? I'm ten years older than him, and he's a glorious man.* His granite-hard body, the broad expanse of his shoulders. Blond hair lightly covered his chest. Rivulets of water ran over his pecks… She wanted to run her hands along him. His cock grew, and she groaned, "No."

He leered at her. Angela held back a shiver.

"My hands are clean now. Come, let me clean you," he said in husky French.

"I'm not dirty." She spoke Italian, refusing to speak French even though she was fluent.

He smiled, and his eyes touched her, making her heart skip a beat. She stood still.

His voice sounded gentle when he said, "I know you're not." Andre moved to stand behind her in the large black marble and glass shower. He rubbed his hands on her breasts, touching his lips to her ear. He said, "Your tits are beautiful and big for one so petite, but not too much for my hands." See, he said, cupping her breasts before he gently squeezed her nipples.

Angela held her breath as they grew pointed, excited.

"So responsive," he said, and his teeth grazed her neck. Andre splayed his fingers as he slid his hand down over her stomach. "Spread your legs," he whispered into her ear. The shower spray rained gentle water on her body as his hand slipped lower, touching her above her mound. Her feet moved apart.

"Nice, Angela, you're going to love what I'm going to do." He sucked on the skin of her neck as he slipped his finger into her. His other hand moved down. She was surrounded by him, the solid wall of his hard body against her back.

She sucked in her breath.

He rubbed her clit with one finger of his other hand. "So big, nice, and slippery." The finger he had in her vagina swirled and pushed deeper. Her hands moved on his forearms; he pressed his hard shaft against her spine. "Face the wall… and lift your knees on the bench."

She stiffened in defiance. Andre pressed on her clit. She bent her head forward as he surrounded her small frame with his hard body and his arms. "Are you fighting me or your own arousal, wildcat?" He thrust a second finger into her, crooking them. "I can reach your G-spot so easily like this." He moved his fingers, and she loved the zaps of pleasure he forced from her. He was so good as he thrust them in and out of her, then he rubbed her clit.

She moaned, leaning against him. Her heart pounded, almost drowning out his voice.

"Pussycat, kneel on the bench, and I'll make you come." She fought the urge and stayed still as he slipped a third finger into her slick passage, zapping nerve endings. He plucked on her clit and pushed his three middle fingers deeper.

"Why must you fight this?" he said.

She didn't know why she fought him. Before she knew what she did, she lifted one knee onto the ledge. Andre steadied her while she lifted her other knee.

"Here, I'll take the edge off," he said against her ear. He held her clit between his thumb and forefinger while he slid the fingers of his other hand in and out of her. She rose and lowered herself on his hand. "Feel my fingers fucking you, pussycat."

She moaned at his words. Pushing forward, her breasts pressed against the shower wall, her buttocks rubbing his erection. She writhed against him as heat radiated through her. Angela screamed as pleasure consumed her. The spasms deep in her core clutched his fingers.

"Ahh, so nice, so hot dripping wet for me."

She breathed in great puffs of steamy air; her hair was

plastered to her body. She rested her cheek on the cool granite of the shower wall.

He slipped his fingers from her, and she cried out, "No."

Then he pressed the head of his erection into her vagina. She couldn't believe it. She came a second time as he slid into her.

"Oh, pussycat, your cunt is so nice and tight."

Angela pressed her forehead on the shower wall. Groaning, she lifted her buttocks. Andre pushed into her, holding her hips as he pulled out and then thrust to the hilt. He pulled out slowly and thrust in fast again and again. His hands moved to her breasts, fingers exciting her nipples. She moved on him, catching his erection in her. Her inner walls tightened, and she shuddered with another mind-blowing orgasm.

CHAPTER 6

$\mathscr{A}$ndre pistoned into that tight pussy, her orgasm stroking him as he continued, to give her another orgasm almost on top of the one before. His balls tightened, he groaned and grabbed her hips. He couldn't hold back anymore. Andre thrust to the hilt, grinding into her wet heat. His pulsing dick raced to explode, gushing into her. The walls of her vagina caressed him, taking all he had to give.

She screamed, begging him. "Please don't stop. More, Andre more. I love what you do to me."

Does she know what she's saying? He held her hips as she almost collapsed against the seat and the shower wall. His heart pounded. He turned her in his arms. Andre sat on the ledge and held her on his lap, the shower spray soothing them. He kissed her temple and her neck. And he stroked her wet hair. When their breathing returned to normal, he said, "Stand, pussycat, and I'll wash your hair."

"I can wash my own hair." She snapped and grabbed the shampoo from him. She turned her back to him.

"As you wish." He scrubbed his body, his gaze on Angela, admiring the indent of her waist, the flare of her hips, her buttocks. He closed his eyes, a smile on his lips. When they finished, he handed her a towel while he dried himself. He led her back to the bedroom. The bed was turned down, the breakfast dishes gone.

"How long do you plan on keeping me here?"

"As long as it takes," he said.

"Takes for what? Oh, you pout like a child."

"You won't provoke me, Angela. I see your game. I'll have you for as long as I want. Tell me that you don't like my filthy hands on you. Do you know what you screamed in the shower?"

She spun around in all her naked glory, black hair damp from the shower flew around her shoulders. Her beautiful breasts with their nipples extended and pink from his kisses swayed. The patch of black hair covering her sex excited him more than the women who shaved their pussies. Her intoxicating taste… he couldn't get enough. Onyx eyes shot fire at him. "When will you give me my clothes?"

"The mourning garb you've worn is gone. No black while you're here. I prefer bright colors on you. For now, the two robes I gave you are enough."

She stamped her foot at him and growled, "Aggr… you are—" She stopped when he took a step toward her. Her gaze fell on his erection.

"Yes, pussycat, I want you again. Get on the bed."

"You'll have to tie me."

"The ties were for your benefit; I can hold you and make you beg me again." He took a step towards her.

"No."

He didn't bother to answer. Picking her up, he carried her the short distance to his bed. Her fists pounded wherever they reached. He dropped her face down on the bed and lay on top of her squirming body. "Stop struggling."

"I hate you."

He reached under her, cupping a breast in his hand. His mouth at her ear, he said, "This is good too." He shoved a knee between her legs and then his other knee. He spread her thighs, lifting her hips. "See how nice and easy this is for me."

"Oh, I—"

"Hate me."

"Yes, I hate you!" she screamed at him.

"I like your taste on my tongue." He flipped her over onto her back with no effort at all.

"What?"

He dragged her to the edge of the bed. She kicked at him, but he slipped off the bed and knelt on the floor. He held her legs still, spreading them as he wedged his shoulders between her thighs. Angela rose on her elbows, her head thrown back. Andre nuzzled the inside of her thigh as he kept her spread for his pleasure. He would make her beg before he satisfied this wildcat.

He dropped kisses on her strip of black curls. The scent of her desire filled his head. He separated the tuft of jet-black hair with his thumbs, kissing her deep in her wet center.

She gasped.

Andre snaked his tongue into her, holding her open. He thrust his tongue in, licked at the walls of her vagina, tasting her sweet lust. He slipped his tongue around to her clit. She trembled in his arms. He sucked on her clit before he pressed his tongue over the whole of it.

She whimpered.

He wouldn't relent, pressing his face into her, applying pressure to her clit, licking her folds.

"*O santo cielo,*" she moaned.

He rubbed a finger at her opening; she lifted her hips, and he pushed two fingers into her.

"Ahhh, *si,* Andre."

He waited until she lay back. Andre knew the moment before she was going to climax, by the sounds she always made. He stopped. Taking his mouth and hands from her.

She tossed her head, whimpered, "Andre... *o Dio*."

He kissed her inner knee and up her thigh. Andre brushed his lips over her petal soft folds. Her fingers combed through his hair. "*O Dio mio*."

She may be a master at manipulation, but I can make her beg. He slowly opened her to his mouth.

Angela held back the moan that built up in her as Andre kissed her sex. Long, lingering kisses sprinkled with shorter ones. She was primed for whatever he wanted her to do, beg, plead, anything he wanted. She gripped the cool sheets to stop her hands from reaching for his head again.

Open-mouthed kisses skimmed across her skin, down to her knee. His tongue licked her inner thigh as he'd done to her other and kissed up her leg. He held her ankles, bending her knees as he lifted her feet to the mattress.

She was so open to him, and nothing mattered but him satisfying the ache he created in her. His big hands held her buttocks, fingers splayed as he massaged her while he used his thumbs to rub her outer lips, opening her.

His blond head between her legs, Andre gazed into her eyes while his mouth moved on her, in her. Heat coiled through Angela, making her vagina pulse. He spread her wider and dipped his tongue into her, thrusting in the way his big cock did. He reached her G-spot before he licked up to her clit. She knew what he would do before he did; he put his lips around the base and used his tongue to lash her clit. She couldn't take her eyes from his silver gaze as he sucked her clit.

Angela couldn't stop the moan that escaped her, and her

head fell back at the intense pleasure. He sucked harder. She looked into his pewter eyes, moving her hips, desperate for him to give her release. Andre teased at her folds, his tongue never entering. She moved to capture his head, and he stopped again. Taking his mouth from her.

She groaned, her body arched, and her core burned with need. Finally, she cried out, "Please."

Andre said nothing as he spread her wider, and then his mouth was where she needed it most, licking, kissing, sucking every part of her. She reached to hold his head to her as her feet dug into his broad shoulders, and her hips moved uncontrollably, her sex against his mouth.

The fire of his lashing tongue stroking her G-spot pushed her over the edge. She came in waves of unending pleasure.

Andre rose from his knees, slipped his hands under her buttocks, and lifted her hips. His massive cock pressed at her entrance. Sliding the engorged head in, he stopped, and she looked into his eyes. What did she see in the depths of his silver gaze? A mix of anger and something else. Angela didn't care. She needed what he gave. "Do you want me to say fuck my pussy?"

He smiled at her. "I like when you talk dirty." He nudged forward.

Angela reached for his steel biceps, her fingers curled around his taught muscles, and she pulled him to her. "Andre, fuck… my… pussy."

He thrust to the hilt. "Ahh… *Dio si, si.*" She met his moves, needing the deep penetration. She climaxed again, holding him to her. Her fingers pressed his body to her, his scent filled her head. She writhed against him, and he stopped when the last wave of her climax ended. He pistoned into her repeatedly. She was insatiable as he brought her to the brink twice more before his hot seed filled her. She was boneless in a euphoric haze of hedonistic pleasure when

Andre moved her to the center of his bed and wrapped himself around her.

They slept until the late afternoon. He woke Angela up, kissing her breasts, her neck, anything but her lips. He hadn't kissed her mouth since the time he did and then became angry. Now he ran his mouth over her body. He turned her over and kissed down her spine to her buttocks. "Your skin is so smooth like satin," he breathed against her before he nipped a buttock. Then he kissed where he'd nipped before he spread her buttocks and ran his tongue over her.

"No." she gasped and squirmed away.

He chuckled and moved on down, kissing the backs of her legs to the soles of her feet. He rose up her body and turned her in his arms. "No one has ever kissed you or licked you where I did?"

"No! There has only been my husband… and he didn't…" Her voice trailed away. Angela couldn't finish the sentence. She knew her face was flushed.

"I've never wanted to with anyone but you, *ma belle*." He leaned against the headboard, pulling her up to rest her back against his chest. He brushed her hair from her face and kissed her temple. "Would you like to soak in the jacuzzi?"

"If you mean alone without you, then yes, I would."

"One day, you'll beg me… oh but you have; yes, you have." His brilliant smile filled her with warmth, even though his words were meant to antagonize.

She tugged at his arm. Angela felt the chuckle deep in his chest.

"Okay, don't struggle so. Yes, alone, I have some contracts I must go over. Then we can have dinner."

"Give me my clothes."

"I like you naked, but maybe… I'll surprise you with something to wear."

"Nothing see-through. Now let me go relax."

He held her to him, his hand caressing her belly. "Would you like some champagne and chocolate?"

Her brows came together, then she smiled. "Truffles? I like hazelnut truffles."

"Yes, you shall have them." He dragged her against his rock-hard body and lifted the receiver from the phone on the nightstand. "Send up a bottle of champagne, the Perignon Brut Rose and some truffles, hazelnut." He put the phone down. "Go and fill the tub. When the champagne arrives, I'll bring it in to you." His knuckles grazed her cheek as he bent to kiss her temple.

ANGELA RELAXED IN THE WHIRLPOOL, letting the warm water ease her muscles. Closing her eyes, she wondered how she would convince Andre to send her back home. She thought of his kiss and how gentle he'd been, coaxing a response from her. Opening herself completely to his lips, his tongue. She'd never felt the way he'd made her feel with his kiss… Then something happened, and he became almost cruel. *Why?* She didn't understand that. *Okay, I used him, big deal. He didn't know I set him up with that woman who looked like Liz, arranged for her to take pictures of the two of them in bed. I used those photos to break up Ricardo and Liz. Then I used Andre to buy stocks to take over my nephew's company, to destroy him.* She rested her head against the rim of the tub, letting the water soothe her.

Angela picked up a truffle from the sterling silver tray. She bit into the chocolate and let the soft center rest on her tongue; her tastebuds came alive with the delicious flavor. She took a sip of the champagne and finished the chocolate. "Ahh, so good." She closed her eyes, and her lips rose into a smile as she thought of Andre. His punishment wasn't so bad… he was great in bed, better than her husband—What! She sat up in the bathtub, water sloshing onto the marble floor. *How? Oh God. How? I feel lust, just lust, nothing more. That dirty bastard. I must get away from him.*

~

ANDRE ENJOYED TEASING HER, using her. He'd been in love once, and now all he wanted was a willing body—or some- what willing—as in Angela's case. He was ruthless, but her kisses could make him forget his anger and almost wish for her love to replace the emptiness, but he didn't need the emotional baggage that went along with love.

They both shared the pain of loss and dealt with it in their own way. She—Andre couldn't believe that Angela hadn't been with a man since her husband died twenty-five years ago.

He, on the other hand, threw himself into work and mindless relationship after mindless relationship. His dick enjoyed being in a woman's mouth or in a wet pussy. He forced Angela into the same category.

Her kisses had stopped him—maybe it would be different with her. That kiss was more than he'd expected. She opened her soul to him. He muttered under his breath and turned away. *Focus on the business at hand.* He sighed and leafed through the hundred-odd pages of the contract. Signed it and moved on to the next. He sat back in his chair and pinched the bridge of his nose. Then he moved on to the next contract. When he finished, he placed the stack in his desk drawer. He lifted the receiver on his desk phone; the line rang directly in James' office.

"The contracts are in my desk drawer. Have them deliv- ered to the New York office. Bring my car around. My guest will remain in my bedroom. Send up Danielle should she require anything." He placed the receiver back on its cradle. He listened as Angela moved around his bedroom.

Andre found her sitting in a wing chair before the fire, her shapely legs curled under her. The sheer forest-green robe caressed her shoulders. Angela had taken a cashmere throw to wrap around her. The fire sizzled and crackled while she ran her fingers through her hair, using the heat to dry the lush jet-black mass.

"I have to go out before dinner, and you'll have to remain here. I apologize for having to lock you in my bedroom again."

Her fingers stilled in her hair, and she gazed up at him. "Oh, how civil you are. Apology not accepted. How long will you be gone?"

"Will you miss me?"

"No, it will be a relief not to have you constantly pawing me."

"Is that what I do? Should you need anything, use the interior phone. James will pick up, and Danielle will bring you whatever you need."

"All I want is my freedom and my clothes!"

Andre ignored her and said, "When I get back, we can have a late dinner and perhaps watch a movie."

She rose from the seat, wrapped the throw around her shoulders, and strolled past him with a sneer on her full lips. "Watch a movie? What am I? A child? I don't watch movies. I go to the theater, the symphony, the opera."

He forced himself not to grab her, hold her against him, and devour her mouth. "Is that so? Maybe we can come to some sort of agreement."

She spun around to gaze into his eyes. "What kind of agreement?"

"We can stay together as you promised with some small amount of freedom. You won't need to be confined to the bedroom. I'll take you to a concert. We can go out… if you gave me your word—"

"You kidnapped me, and now you want me to agree to stay willingly?"

"Yes."

"What do I get?"

"You can have some freedom to walk around the house. I have a gym and an indoor pool. I have a magnificent library. You can read a book, since you don't like movies. But no phone or computer."

She did the cutest American accent when she said, "Wow, golly gee whiz, a library…" She flounced back down into the chair by the fire, shrugged a delicate shoulder at him, and said, "Some freedom is better than none. I'll agree with those terms. What about sex?"

My pussycat agreed too quickly. What's she up to? He pretended to misunderstand her and lifted his eyebrows to wiggle at her. "You want to go to bed now?"

"No. I meant—"

A grin tugged the corners of his lips. "I know what you meant, but sex is non-negotiable and off the table… wherever, whenever… and however. Deal, pussycat?"

"Oh, you're *un uomo*—"

He took a step toward her.

She lifted her chin and peered down her nose at him. "Yes, okay. Deal." She quickly agreed.

He liked her spunk and the way she could turn this to her advantage. He couldn't trust her… She was a master manipulator, but her kisses were worth everything to him.

"For now, you'll have to stay in my bedroom until I can get you something more appropriate to wear around the house."

CHAPTER 7

*A*fter her remark about the symphony, Andre surprised her with tickets to a Christmas Eve concert. He ordered some sexy clothes—nothing black—for the vixen whose kisses drove him to lengths he hadn't reached with any other woman. While she bathed, Andre laid out a skintight dress in a deep wine color with a matching bra and thong. Silk stockings, a garter, and silver, red-soled high heels completed the outfit. Next to the outfit, he placed a jeweler's box with diamond earrings. He dressed in a black designer tuxedo and waited for her to come out of the en suite into the dressing room.

She walked in, wrapped in a fluffy white towel. "Oh, real clothes," she said as she dropped the towel from her body. Angela lifted the thong and shrugged. "It isn't much coverage, but it's better than the lousy see-through robes." She'd snarked at him.

"You look beautiful nude as you are," he said.

She stepped into the thong.

"Hurry, wildcat. We don't want to be late." He left her to finish dressing.

Angela walked into the bedroom. She applied eyeliner and mascara to her eyes and put her hair up. The wine-colored dress hugged her curves, stopping just above her knees. The silver heels added inches to her petite form. "Wildcat, I bought this for you," he said as he wrapped a full-length white mink coat over her outfit. He bent his head and brushed the side of her neck with a kiss. Her perfume drifted around him, and he had to pull away, or he would be the reason they would be late. She had accepted the mink without comment, and he noticed her running her fingers along the collar.

Andre's chauffeur waited at the back passenger door of a silver Mercedes, ready to transport them to the concert. When they emerged from the mansion, the driver opened the back door. Andre held her hand and assisted Angela into the backseat. She slid away from him, turning her head, and peered out the window. She'd pinned her hair up but thank God, not in the old ladies' bun she was fond of. A diamond hair comb he had purchased for her strategically held the chignon in place.

His chauffeur brought out two cut-crystal mugs. "Monsieur, I thought you and your lady would like some *Vin Chaud* for the drive."

"Splendid idea, thank you." Andre pulled down the mini table in the console and then accepted both glasses. His driver closed the door. "Wildcat, the French version of mulled wine. Have some. The heater is on, but it's quite cold tonight. We may have a white Christmas."

"I like spiced wine." Angela sipped. "Mmm, nice. I can taste the orange, anise, and cloves."

"It's definitely spicy like you, *ma belle.*"

While they were at the theater, a light snow had fallen. They drove along Champs Elysees. Each of the trees lining the wide avenue was draped with hundreds of red and blue twinkling lights. Colorful decorations adorned the upscale restaurant windows and storefronts along the way. Paris, the city of lights, put on a wonderful display at Christmas.

"Do you think we can drive by the Eiffel Tower? I know we can see it from your home, but can we get a view of the entire structure?"

He wrapped one arm around her, tugged her petite form into him, and kissed her neck.

"Yes, anything you desire." Andre pressed the intercom and asked his driver to take them home but find a place where they could admire the Eiffel Tower from across the park.

When they arrived back at his home, he led her to the formal dining room. A fire was lit in the fireplace and the mahogany dining table was set for an intimate candlelit midnight supper, complete with caviar and champagne. The side board was covered with pastries and cakes in the French tradition of thirteen different desserts. The centerpiece was a yule log filled with her favorite hazelnut chocolate.

They sipped champagne, and Angela tasted a piece of each dessert. "I like the yule log the best. This is definitely a different Christmas Eve than I thought I would have and one I'm happy to have experienced."

"I'm pleased to have given you this and more when we go to bed."

"Oh, I see your plan. Ply me with champagne and these rich desserts so I'll go to bed with you." She dazzled him with her smile before she said, "I guess the secret's out. I have a sweet tooth."

"And a sweet body." Andre took her hand, and she rose from her seat.

They held hands and walked up to his bedroom. Her willingness brought him pleasure he'd never experienced with any other woman. Her raw, wild need drove his lustful desire to the point where he was consumed with a burning urgency for her and only her. He held her in his arms throughout the night.

On Christmas morning, he snuggled Angela to him. "Merry Christmas, Angela." He kissed the warm flesh behind her ear before nibbling on her neck. "Go shower. I have a surprise for you."

She picked her head up. "Are you letting me go? That would be the best gift you could give me."

"Wildcat, after last night… I must work harder… because I thought you agreed I am your everything."

"I agreed to nothing." She threw her legs over the side of the bed, then sauntered into the bathroom.

He followed and leaned a shoulder against the entry frame. "I gave the staff the day off, but they prepared food for us."

"Coffee would be good. Will you get me a cup while I hurry and shower?"

"For you, wildcat, yes. We can sit by the fire and have breakfast."

Andre left Angela to shower while he went down to the kitchen for the coffee. He'd asked his chef to prepare her a special pastry filled with her favorite chocolate. The hazelnut yule log had also been his idea. Andre enjoyed pleasing her with little things. He chuckled. He had a perpetual hard on around her, but he tried to control himself, although she could do the most innocent thing, and he'd be ready. One day, she'd only brushed past him, and he lifted her up, tossed her on the desk, and made glorious love to her.

Andre carried the tray up to his bedroom and shouldered the door open. She stood before the fire in his white silk shirt, toweling dry her lustrous jet-black hair. She turned when he entered. The shirt reached above her knees. She'd rolled the sleeves up above her wrists. *White accents her olive complexion. She's glowing.*

"I hope you don't mind that I took one of your shirts to wear rather than the sheer robe."

"Wildcat, I have come to realize that whatever you wear or don't wear, you're a desirable and sexy woman."

She huffed at him, and he saw the beginning of a blush cover her cheeks.

After breakfast, he brought her the white mink and a pair of shoes. "Come with me to the rooftop terrace. I want to show you Paris covered in a blanket of snow."

"Shouldn't I wear more than your shirt under the coat?"

"*Ma belle*, I'll keep you warm." They climbed the interior stairs to the terrace.

"It's truly beautiful and magical." She huddled in her coat, with only his silk shirt and heels on. The wind blew the powdery snow through the air. She shivered.

"You're cold, so let's go back inside," he said as he wrapped his arms around her.

"No, Andre, a moment more, please." Her gaze held his.

Andre pushed a thick strand of her lustrous black hair from her cheek, tucking it behind her ear. "Okay," he said as he kissed the tip of her nose.

She spread her hand over the view. "This is so beautiful. I've never been to Paris when it snowed. Venice, yes, but never Paris. This is breathtaking."

"I love the view from up here, but it's freezing and windy now. Let's go in, *ma belle*."

Christmas Day passed pleasantly in bed, with him being gentle and almost loving. At one point, he'd asked her if she knew how to play backgammon or chess. "Can we bet, if I win, you'll send me home?"

"What will you give me if I win?" He trailed his fingers on her arm, drawing patterns on her delicate skin.

"You've already taken everything."

He wanted a firmer commitment from her not to go but decided to go slowly, not completely trusting her. "Not quite, I want you... willing... always."

"No, thanks. I don't want to bet."

He laughed. "The chessboard is set up in my study." She was a good strategist, but he'd been world champion at a young age.

She won the first two games and smiled at him. "I should have bet you."

"We still can, *ma belle*."

Her gaze caught his. She pursed her lips. He could almost see her contemplation, and then she said, "No, you're too eager, and I fear lulling me into a false sense of security."

"We'll never know, now will we... Tell me, how did you spend Christmas when you were younger?"

She leaned back in her chair. "When Salvatore was alive, he loved to decorate the villa and follow all the Christmas traditions. We made it a priority to be home in Sicily and get together with his mother and my brother and his family. Sometimes, all the families and extended families would be at our villa, but mostly at my brother's palazzo. He has a ballroom, and we would dance the night away." A wistful smile touched her lips.

He saw the nostalgia in her dark-as-night eyes before they filled with sadness.

"After Sal died... Giorgio was young, so I forced myself to decorate, be festive for him. I tried to make the holiday memorable for my son. Some years, we went to New York City to see the Christmas show at Radio City, the tree at Rockefeller Center, and ice skating at The Rink under the tree. If we didn't go to New York, we'd go skiing in the Alps." Angela shook her head and lifted a shoulder, then she said,

"Anything to get away. But you can't run away from your memories."

"When my wife was alive, we would always spend Christmas in Paris. Go to Midnight Mass at Notre Dame, stay up until six in the morning, and then sleep all of Christmas Day, before we went out with our family in the evening."

Angela picked up her head and stared into his eyes. "Is this… the home where…" Her voice trailed away.

"Adrianna wanted her niece to have the house we lived in. It's in a trust for her. I bought this house as an investment six months ago—" He frowned. "Did you think—you are the only woman who has ever been in this bed with me."

She was willing, and Andre wanted to find out where this would lead. He'd always been attracted to her and wanted to take her to bed from the first time they'd met. She was the one who rejected his advances; she felt he was too young. But he was only ten years younger and now, at thirty-nine and forty-nine, age no longer mattered.

When he'd stripped her and found that sexy body under the widow black clothes, he couldn't control his desire for her. Now her kisses and her hot pussy were all he thought about. To have her willing and available after all the struggling made him blind to the possibility she had ulterior motives. *After all, she used me to try to take over her nephew's company, and she had manipulated me into believing Liz wanted me—damn, the way she played me like a game of chess—making me believe it was Liz. When Ricardo had confronted me with the photos—I didn't know I'd been photographed—and the woman who I picked up in The Champagne Bar in New York City thinking it was Liz was a damn good look-a-like.*

The day after Christmas, they ate breakfast in his bedroom by the fire. "Would you like to go for a swim in the pool?" he casually asked.

She put her fork down and frowned at him, shaking her head. "Not naked."

"Hmm, so you want to wear perhaps a bathing suit?" He reached under his chair and handed her a gift box, wrapped in red and green paper with a huge gold bow placed in the center.

She opened the box and, pushing the delicate golden tissue paper to the side, lifted out a white bathing suit. Holding it by the thin shoulder straps, she looked at the one-piece suit. "Wow, more coverage than I expected. I'm going to put it on right now." She ran to the en suite.

Andre smiled, happy with his gift. He put on his bathing trunks. When she came out of the en suite, Angela had tied her hair back from her face, and the suit was perfection on her. The thin straps at her shoulders, the white suit clung to her big breasts, and the huge cutouts accented her small waist with the roundness of her hips. The high V made her legs look longer. She twirled around before him, the curve of her buttocks so enticing. He lifted her into his arms.

She looped her arms around his neck, resting her head on his shoulder. "I can't wait to see this pool you rave about."

"It's downstairs." Andre carried her down to the lower level. He shouldered open an antique arched wooden door.

"Oh my, this is fabulous. You said you had a pool, but I never imagined anything like this."

"When the real estate agent sent me the photos of this house, the pool sold me. It's like a grotto."

"I love to swim. Wherever I am, that has always been a constant in my life."

They spent the morning swimming, and then Andre called James to have lunch set up poolside. Champagne fizzed in crystal flutes. White ceramic individual crocks were filled with onion soup, a crusty toasted baguette, and gruyere cheese melted across the top and down the sides. Dessert was macaroons filled with raspberry rose buttercream and a cup of espresso.

"I think we should christen the swimming pool... Have you ever made love in a pool, *ma belle?*"

"No, I haven't... Suppose one of your staff comes in? Andre, no."

He stepped out of his swim trunks, his cock stretched up to his abdomen. "No one will come in."

"*O Dio.*" She peeled her bathing suit off, and he lifted her into the water.

That night, he took her out to dinner at Maxim's. They ate in a private area of the famous restaurant and then went to the main floor to watch a show. Once back in his car, Andre assured her that the backseat of his limousine afforded every privacy, and the driver would never know if they were making love. "I'm not taking my clothes off. Suppose we get pulled over or worse, we're in an accident?"

"My driver is careful; there isn't any chance of being stopped."

"I don't want to take a chance. We'll be home soon."

He smiled. "Do you know this is the first time you have referred to my house as home?"

"Don't let it go to your head."

Andre took her hand and put it on his groin. His gaze held hers in the semidarkness of his limousine.

"I can feel that it's too late. Andre, I won't get undressed," she said.

"You don't have to but spread your legs for me." His fingers and his mouth found her desire.

THE FOLLOWING NIGHT, they had dinner at home. "Do you like to dance?"

"I don't dance, not since my husband… It's too painful of a memory."

"You've mourned more than enough. Do you think he'd be happy with the way you closed yourself off?"

"It's my business how I handle my grief. The subject is off limits." She shoved her chair back and stormed from the dining room.

Andre understood and didn't force the issue, but he would get her out dancing before too long. He left the dining room and followed her upstairs.

THE WEEK between Christmas and New Year, they spent going out for dinner, the theater, or staying home. No matter what, the night always ended with them making love. They christened more than just the pool, and he taught her that there were many ways and positions to make love in. He never mentioned dancing again.

It was late in the afternoon on New Year's Eve when Andre awoke. Angela slept in his arms, draped over him, one shapely leg over his hip. He tugged her to him, his lips at the base of her throat as he kissed her. She stretched her lethal body against him, wrapping her arms around his shoulders.

In a sleep-filled voice, she said, "I should be at my nephew's wedding tonight." She spread her fingers, playing with the hair on his chest before rubbing her hand along the mat of hair, trailing her finger down his abdomen.

"I enjoy having you here at my beck and call, for my pleasure." He growled, molding her to him. Her big breasts dug into his chest, arousing him. "Get dressed, we can take a walk."

She stiffened in his arms. He brushed his lips against her temple, whispering, "I didn't mean that as it sounded." *Your body excites the hell out of me and what your fingers are doing.* "Would you like to go for a walk?"

"That would be nice, an afternoon stroll through Paris. Then what I want is to go home, back to Palermo."

"Let's not argue. Wear the pretty new thong I bought you under your dress."

"The one with the pearls and no coverage at all? I—"

"Yes, wildcat; it's my gift to you."

She rose from the bed and walked to the dressing room. Andre watched as her black hair swung loosely down her back. Her firm buttocks moved with each step she took.

"I can help you dress." *Have a quickie against the wall.*

She laughed but continued walking into the dressing room. "If you helped me dress, I know we'd never go for that walk."

"Would you mind that, wildcat?"

"No. Maybe later, we can go for a swim. I can wear the other bathing suit you bought me."

She walked out of the dressing room in a burgundy dress that hugged her curves. Angela wore black leather knee-high stiletto boots instead of high-heel pumps. Her hair hung in waves around her shoulders. Angela accented her eyes with eyeliner and mascara and applied berry-colored lipstick to her full lips. The slight indent in the center of her bottom lip beckoned him.

He'd dressed in the bedroom, putting on a fresh shirt and tie while she was in the dressing room. "You're beautiful. I like the choice of boots."

She walked up to him, leaned her body into his, and caressed his cheek. "You're a very handsome man."

He breathed in her orange blossom scent. "Are you wearing the pearl thong?" At her nod, Andre took Angela's delicate hand, turned it palm up, and brought his lips to the center. He kissed her soft skin, then touched his tongue on the spot he'd kissed.

She pulled her hand away. "Oh, you're impossible."

"I know, *ma belle*. I won't tease you. Some fresh air will be good for both of us." He picked up her mink and helped her into it, then he grabbed his black cashmere coat. They walked out of the house and barely down the street to the Eiffel Tower. He watched closely for her reaction to the thong. Her step faltered, then she took two more steps before she suddenly stopped walking and looked up at him. The accusation in her obsidian eyes confirmed the pearls had begun their intimate massage. "You're a degenerate."

He bent down to whisper near her ear, "How's that? Is something happening between your beautiful legs? Tell me, are you wetting the pearls yet?"

"Oh, you pig—"

"It's just a few more streets to—"

She groaned and swayed toward him.

"Shall we go back?"

She didn't answer, but her lids slid over her black eyes, her berry-tinted lips parted, and her cheeks held a hint of a blush.

Raw, wild need settled in his groin, and he held her tiny waist for a heartbeat. "Let's go back home," he whispered.

She nodded. As they walked, Angela held her head up high, and he felt the effort it took her not to moan. As they reached the house, he lifted her in his arms and carried her into the foyer. She moaned then, and he couldn't move any further without bending to kiss her lips.

"You are beautiful and I want you now."

She looped her arms tighter around his neck. "Yes… but your staff… Please not in the hall; bring me to your bed instead."

He lifted her high against his chest, carrying Angela up

the stairs. Andre rushed to the bedroom door and shouldered it open. He took a step in, then stood Angela on the floor while he locked the door.

"No one would dare enter this room or any while the door is closed. I remember what happened when Danielle walked into the study while we were… well, you remember."

Angela's cheeks flushed. She slid the coat off her shoulders, and the white mink fell to the floor. She turned her back to him, and he unzipped her dress.

"I didn't want to upset her. I never meant to yell so loud. From now on, we lock doors."

He peeled the dress away from her. Andre could see her nipples pointed through the pink lace cups of her bra. The pink thong with its heart-shape lace rested low, and the string of white pearls between her shapely legs rested in her seam. The pearls glistened with her need. Her stockings and garter with the knee-high black boots drove his flaming desire to new heights.

Andre yanked off his jacket and pulled his tie from his neck, while Angela reached to unbutton his shirt. He unhooked her bra while she unzipped his pants. She reached into his silk boxers and caressed his aroused length.

He lifted her to the middle of the bed, and she lay back against the pillows. Her breasts rising and falling with each excited breath, her nipples puckered and grew.

"Come here, I need you," she said, running her pointing finger along the strand of white pearls nestled between her slightly parted legs.

Mon diu, does she know what she does to me? Andre unzipped her boots, first one and then the other. He dropped them to the floor with a muffled thump against the Persian rug. He rolled her stockings down her legs, tossing them to the floor near the boots, dropping the garter on top of them.

The pearls glistened, and he throbbed. "I have to taste

you." Andre bent from the waist and licked the line of pearls. The pressure of his tongue pressed them into her, and once more licked up her pussy. "Do you wish to go?" He tongued the pearl that rested on her clit.

"Go?" She sounded confused, her fingers playing with his hair.

He breathed in her scent, moving his lips over her as he said, "Yes, you said you wanted to go back to Palermo." He licked the line of pearls again, then his tongue pressed the pearl on her clit once more.

She arched her back. "Ahh Andre, no, not… now; now I want to come."

Andre stripped the thong from Angela. He was so hard as he crawled up over her excited body and kneeled between her spread legs. With his hands on either side of her head, his fingers slipped through the jet-black mass of tangled hair. "*Ma belle.*" He took her mouth, brushing the full, sensuous lips with his, she opened to the demand of his lips so he could plunge his tongue into the sweet taste. He twined his tongue with hers and caught her deep moan in his mouth.

She shifted her head, taking in a deep gulp of breath as she lifted her knees and tilted her pelvis. "Now, Andre."

Angela writhed against him and reached her hand down to guide him to her entrance. "Now, now, fuck my pussy."

Her words drove him, and he thrust into her, burying himself in her heat, the tightness almost sending him over the edge. He fought for control, and then he kissed her breasts, sucked, and nipped at her excited nipples.

Angela lifted her legs to his hips and locked her ankles, holding on to his biceps. "Please," she begged him to go faster and deeper. "*O Dio mio.* Don't stop."

"Never, wildcat." He pumped into her over and over. She screamed the loudest with her third orgasm, and then he abandoned his control, erupting into her tight pussy.

Much later, Andre rose from the bed and wrapped the mink coat around her sated, naked body. He helped her step into a pair of heels and led her up the stairs to the terrace, where they could watch the fireworks show on the Eiffel Tower. Andre wrapped his arms around her, dragging her into his body.

The Eiffel Tower lit up red as white fireworks shot up from the ground through to the top, making a fountain of white starbursts showering down through the air. The tower changed colors from red to white and finally blue. They could hear the music over the popping sounds and cheers from the crowds surrounding the iconic tower.

A mass of people spread out along the streets. The night sky was alive in colors of blue, white, and red starbursts. Some high above and some lower, the sky exploded in an array of color. They were so close that for a moment, Andre and Angela could smell the gunpowder. Andre poured champagne for them, and they toasted the new year.

"Happy New Year, *ma belle*." He bent his head and, taking her lips in a demanding kiss, Angela responded with her own demands. Andre slipped his hands under the coat and onto her naked body. "You're so beautiful, there's no other person I would rather begin the new year with than you, Angela."

She wrapped her arms around his waist, resting her head on his chest. "Dance with me." Andre didn't question her. He swayed to the tune he'd been humming. Angela smiled up at him. "I like to waltz, but I love to tango."

Andre waltzed her around the rooftop terrace five minutes into the new year. "Tomorrow, we can tango. Right now, I want to take you to bed."

IT WAS A NEW YEAR. They sipped champagne while watching the fireworks. For the first time, Angela's thoughts were of Andre and his lovemaking, not what she'd lost when her husband died. Andre waltzed her around the terrace, in just her coat, and naked beneath. Another kiss, and they went back into the house and his bed.

Without any discussion, they fell into a comfortable routine of coffee and a pastry in bed, followed by a morning swim, lunch in his study, and dinner in the formal dining room, or out at a restaurant. She dressed in the clothes he'd bought her. He surprised her with gifts of diamonds, rubies, emeralds, necklaces, and earrings. Sometimes, she'd find the jewelry mixed in with boxes of chocolates and even a bottle of her favorite perfume.

There wasn't any more talk of her going home. He'd asked if she wanted to call her son, but she didn't want to. She didn't want to do anything other than stay with Andre. Love, lust, she needed what he gave her, opening her to sensations she'd kept buried in her.

After their swim, they'd shower and make love. She would stay in bed while Andre worked for a while, or she'd go to his library. It was truly grand. She would read or sit and think. For the first time in her life, her thoughts were in total disarray. One part of her thought that this could be fun for a short time. Had Andre not forced her with his lovemaking, she would never have known what she was missing. It was insane that at her age, she could feel so alive. He kept her young, something she had made shrivel up and die when Salvatore died. Each year, without a man in her life, it became easier to remain celibate.

"Tell me about your husband," Andre asked one day while they ate lunch at an intimate table in the study, far away from his bedroom.

"He and my brother Giuseppe were best friends. They

started DiMarco Enterprises together. My parents didn't want us to marry. They felt I was too young, and his mother didn't want Sal to marry me. She went so far as to say that I turned his head and had ulterior motives. My only motive was love and wanting to spend the rest of my life with him… When he died… I spent hours at his grave. I wouldn't let her come to the cemetery… I don't know why, but I hated her. I never told anyone… I blame her for his death… I would drop Giorgio at school and go to Sal's grave. There were times when I would forget to pick Giorgio up after school, and my brother would take him to his house for me."

Angela took an uneven breath and rubbed the back of her neck before she continued, "I was so confused. Sal had insisted the company name should be DiMarco Enterprises to honor me, but after he died, my brother said that I couldn't have a place in the company because I was a woman. I worried Giorgio would lose his inheritance."

"But that didn't happen. I thought your brother insisted Giorgio be trained along with his sons."

"Yes, I know, but when Ricardo became CEO, I felt like he had overstepped my son." She stood from her seat and sauntered around the table to Andre. "Now, I'm here with you." She laid his hand against her breasts. Angela gazed into his silver eyes and said, "I may as well make the best of it."

"Yes, we most definitely should, *ma belle*." He slid his chair back, and she straddled him, slipping her hands around his neck.

"This morning after breakfast, we were interrupted with that phone call."

"Yes, my brother Jacques will be in New York. He's flying in from Australia next week, and he wanted me to meet him."

She brushed the pads of her fingers through the short, blond hair at the back of his nape, every now and again scraping her nails on his neck. He pulled her forward on his lap.

"And..." She held his cheeks between her hands and ran her thumb along his bottom lip, in a similar way that he'd always done to her. Then she tilted her head, parting her lips to press over his. She could feel him swell with his arousal. *I can get him excited so easily.*

He trailed his fingers along the hem of her dress, moving the fabric up her legs and exposing her thighs before he cupped her buttocks and brought her close against his muscled body. She kissed him, using every skill she could think of while she unbuttoned his shirt.

CHAPTER 8

*A*ngela worked at lulling him into a false sense of security. *I won't fall in love with him, but I'm going to take this time and enjoy his glorious body.* She swore to herself that she'd never fall in love again, and especially not with a younger man. No matter how he woke her to lust. He taught her about these primitive desires that she'd never dreamed of. Her hedonistic side loved the way his cock could bring her multiple orgasms. *If life were only sex... but it's not.*

He'd treated her like the spoils of war. She was a manipulator and knew that once he felt avenged, he'd leave her, so she had to get away from him first. *Lust is not love, and once he's satisfied, this will be over.* She'd been independent for far too long. Angela didn't know what love was or if she could give herself over to that emotion ever again. She remembered the constant pain. She wouldn't chance that type of sorrow again. No, she wouldn't.

Now that she had some clothes and a little more freedom to walk around the house, she'd found some money in his desk drawer and hid it between her breasts to hide the euros in the dressing room wardrobe. Angela thought she'd been caught hiding the money when he walked into the dressing room. She ran to him and kissed him, throwing herself into his arms and taking his mind off her as she led him to the bed.

They'd spent hours in bed, making love, and then Andre called to have dinner ready for them in the dining room. Angela slipped on an outfit that he had given her a few days ago. She prided herself on her powers of manipulation and how easily she could lull Andre into a false sense of love. She didn't love him, but she certainly enjoyed the lust he aroused in her. He whetted her appetite for sex, wanting and needing him, but certainly not love.

ANDRE SUSPECTED she'd been up to something when he walked into the dressing room. He was certain she hid something in the wardrobe, by the way she jumped and put her hand behind her back. *I knew better than to believe her and her lies. I want her at my mercy!* Later that night, while Angela slept, he found the money she'd hidden. Andre decided he wouldn't confront her now. Soon… but not quite at this moment. He had a plan.

A few days later, they sat in the formal dining room having dinner. His chef made one of her favorite meals. Angela had met with the man and explained what she wanted. Pasta alla Norma: pasta, eggplant, and a fresh tomato sauce with grated cheese.

Andre couldn't help but admire her beauty in the red velvet cocktail dress that he'd bought her. The boat neck barely hugged her shoulders, and she'd combed her hair to one side and fastened it with one of the many hair orna-ments he'd ordered for her. Her jet-black hair curled over one bare shoulder and down over her breast. She wore a diamond and ruby necklace, earrings, and matching bracelet he'd given her at Christmas.

"Wildcat, tonight, will you wear the sheer white robe with the marabou for me?"

"If you want me to, I will."

"Wear the diamond choker as well. I want to see them against your olive complexion."

THEY SAT on the velvet settee by the crackling fire in his bedroom. He'd poured them each a brandy. She in the sheer robe, Andre wore a black silk robe. He rested against a bolster while she curled onto his side. Andre played with her hair, slipping the silky strands through his fingers, and then he stroked her breasts. Angela touched his lips with her fingertip, her black eyes holding his gaze.

Andre groaned inwardly, knowing what he planned, but he had to take her mouth in a kiss. Bending, his lips brushed hers slowly and leisurely. He traced the soft fullness of her lips with his tongue. The taste of brandy inflamed him, and Angela wrapped her arms around his neck, pressing her breasts into his hands. The half-empty glasses of liquor were left on the end table.

His mouth slanted over hers, capturing her sighs. He kissed the satin smooth flesh behind her ear. He was as hard as a rock. His voice came in a gruff whisper, "The jewels were a gift for you, and I have a gift for me. I was going to wait, and we could have discussed this, but I'm not sure… how long before you succeed, wildcat, in evading my hospitality."

She moved her head, gazing into his eyes. "What—"

"I want you to wear this when I fuck your mouth." He

picked up a package from beside the sofa and opened the box to reveal a pink vibrator and remote control.

Her eyes rounded, and he saw panic in their depths. "What is it?"

"It's a very special vibrator… Have you never used one?"

She shook her head. "No."

"You'll like it, wait and see." He leaned back on the sofa. "Come stand in front of me."

She wouldn't move. Many of their most enjoyable times began with her being stubborn, so he nudged her forward.

"Andre, don't do this."

He ignored her and looped his fingers into the satin belt before he tugged her from the sofa to stand between his feet. He couldn't resist pressing a kiss on her abdomen, breathing in her fragrance, orange blossom, and her unique female scent. The memory of her taste lingered on his tongue, branding him.

Angela stood tense, and he searched her eyes. "Let me see if you're wet enough. I don't want you to be uncomfortable." As he spoke, he moved his hand under her robe and traced the narrow tuft of soft, jet-black curls along the seam. His middle finger slid past the folds of her inner lips and into her vagina. "Andre—"

"No talking, you're nice and slick." He attached the strap to the vibrator, and with the remote, he tested the rabbit ears. They moved, and he heard her gasp.

"I'll always hate you for this," she hissed.

He didn't answer her. Instead, he said, "Remove your robe and give me the tie."

"You'll have to do it. I will not help you in this madness."

He tugged one end of her satin belt and untied the bow. Then he slipped the material and pulled the belt through the loops. He put it on the sofa next to him. Holding the marabou-trimmed robe, he spread the filmy fabric open and slipped it from her beautiful body. Looking at her naked, her high breasts rose and fell with her breath. Angela had an amazing body.

Aroused and throbbing with need, Andre smiled at her. "See what you do to me? I can't wait for you to take me into that heavenly mouth of yours. Spread your legs."

She groaned. "What will that do?"

Is that panic or excitement I hear in her voice? "I'm going to put this into your pussy, and then these will rest against your clit and simulate a tongue."

"You're depraved."

He grabbed her waist and brought her forward. "I know." He held the vibrator at her entrance, not wanting to hurt her as he slowly slid it into place. She gasped. Then he secured the belt behind her at the small of her back. "Is that okay?"

"Disgratziato."

"I guess it's good. Now on your knees." She shook her head. He tapped the remote.

"Oh."

"That's the lowest setting, *ma belle*. Kneel."

Angela stood without moving, her big breasts heaving. She compressed her lips, her jaw set, and her eyes shot daggers at him. She was captivating in her refusal. He wanted her to submit. Andre raised the setting a notch. "Kneel."

"Never again will I get on my knees to you."

He turned on the rabbit ears.

She swayed. "Oh… you are—"

"Kneel, Angela. Your nipples are getting excited. I can see how nicely they are extending, needing my mouth to suck them. How is your clit feeling?"

"You're depraved."

"Do as I say."

She growled at him, shaking her head. "No."

"I found the money you hid. I know you're trying to run, and I'll have this before you go."

He added the G-spot stimulator. Angela stood before him, her body undulated, and a soft moan escaped her parted lips.

He rose to his feet. She held her head high, and he stared into her obsidian eyes. He could see by the stubborn set of her jaw that she refused to be intimidated by him. *Fool that I am, to think she would ever cower.* Andre breathed in her orange blossom scent. He bent his head to her breasts, licking and wetting first one nipple, then the other. He rubbed his thumbs over the damp, puckered flesh, circling the areolae, brushing the excited nipples with the pads of his thumbs.

She moaned louder and swayed toward him with her eyes closed. "Ah, ahh, yes." He nibbled on her breasts and waited another second before he turned off the vibrator.

Her eyes flew open, fury blazed in the black depths. He gave her a half smile and lifted a brow at her. "Will you kneel?"

She shook her head. "No."

A grin tugged at his lips and again, he touched the remote, turning on the vibrator. He drew her into his embrace, cupped her head, and bent, taking her lips with his. He coaxed her lips apart, and Angela rose on her toes, fitting into his body. She opened her mouth to his demands. He nibbled on the corner of her mouth, sucking her bottom lip into his mouth before he breathed against her lips. "Shall I raise the setting on the vibrator and make you orgasm like this in my arms?"

She shoved at his chest. "Ohhh you *disgratziato—*"

He dragged her into his arms, kissing her lips, her neck, her heaving breasts. Her fingers slid into his hair, and her moan filled the room. He lifted his head and taking his lips from her body, he said, "How about now? Will you kneel?" Once more, he brought her to the brink of orgasm and prevented her release. "I'll keep denying you an orgasm until you kneel." He almost gave in. She was ravishing in her defiance.

She groaned, "Know that I'll always hate you for what you're doing to me." Angela slowly sank to her knees between his feet.

Andre sat back down on the settee and spread his black silk robe open. "Oh pussycat, you're going to love what this will do to your cunt, and I'm going to love the feel of your orgasms while my dick is down your throat."

He picked up the white satin belt and tied her hair back from her face; he stroked the diamonds at her neck. "We'll start at a lower setting. Take me in your hand and use your tongue. If you please me, I'll make you come." She inched forward on her knees, and he spread his thighs so she could get closer.

He couldn't wait and took her face in his hands. Andre ran his thumb along her bottom lip, swollen and wet from his kisses, back and forth, then he pressed the pad of his thumb on the slight indent in the center. "Oh pussycat, open your lips and take me into your lovely, lying mouth."

ANGELA WAS SO excited by what he did. *Dio mio, a vibrator!* How it made her feel as zaps of sheer desire flooded her. How could she reach such a high state of excitement? When he'd turned on the rabbit ears, she couldn't believe how that stimulation made her clit burn with desire, and the sucking sensation was almost as good as when Andre sucked her clit.

Then, *o Dio, the G-spot stimulation,* when the vibrator

moved against her just like his fingers did, she couldn't resist the pulsing climax that snuck up on her.

She'd accused him of being depraved, but so was she. Now on her knees between his spread thighs, she wanted to please him. She'd learned so much in the weeks he kept her here. Now she did what he wanted, reaching for his glorious male length. The engorged head seeped pre-come. She licked the velvety smooth skin with the flat of her tongue, tasting him as she spread his essence over his shaft.

Angela began at the base of the long, thick length, lashing her tongue along up to the head, taking him into her mouth before she lashed her tongue down to the base and again up the thick length. Angela stopped to trace a vein up the side of his magnificent cock.

When she reached the head, this time she touched the ridge on the underside with the tip of her tongue, back and forth. She kept her tongue on that sensitive spot until he groaned. Under her long, dark lashes, she gazed up into his silver eyes as she took him into her mouth. "Yes, pussycat, suck my dick into your hot mouth."

She did.

"Oh yes, that's it… Here is your reward."

The rabbit ears and the G-spot stimulator came on. She held his muscular thigh with one hand. A moan escaped her. With her other hand, she pumped his thick length the way he'd shown her.

His long fingers pressed on her head, and she took more of his length into her mouth. Angela looked up at him in time to see a smile spread across his lips.

He raised the setting on the vibrator and cupped her head, holding her down while he lifted his hips. At the first pulsing zing of her orgasm, she forced her throat to relax, taking more of him into her mouth. The sex toy on her pussy made her sizzle with sensation as a climax ripped through her. Andre filled her mouth, slipping down her throat. Angela's scream of hedonistic pleasure was lost around his cock.

"Oh, pussycat, yes, come. The feel of your hot mouth so full of me, and the shudders of your orgasm are vibrating up my dick, through my body."

Her moans were lost in her throat. But she knew he could feel them as he held her head on him, his fingers twining in her hair. "Breathe through your nose, *ma belle*." The speed of the vibrator increased. She held onto his thighs, her nails digging into the muscles. "Nice," he said, "Pussycat, are you coming again?"

She couldn't answer with her mouth full of him.

"Yes, you are… ahh so… good."

His breathing sounded labored, with deep, quick breaths, "Ah ahh, pussycat." He shifted his hips in little thrusting movements. His fingers dug into her hair, raising and lowering her head on him.

Her clit was on fire. The orgasms came one on top of the other. Through the haze of her excitement, she heard him.

"When I come, you're going to swallow all of me." He pushed her head down at the same time he thrust his hips up. She breathed through her nose, taking him down her throat. He held her on him, lifting his hips. His shaft throbbed in her mouth, and the vibrator was relentless, bringing her to another orgasm.

He gritted through his teeth, "Yes, so damn good." He inched out of her throat. "Oh *Cherie*, suck my dick."

She did and at the same time, her own shuddering waves of climax took her by storm. He held her head down and lifted his hips, then he groaned as his hot come filled her mouth.

"Swallow," he said.

She did. Her heart raced as his cock laid on her tongue,

and the vibrator sent waves of bliss sizzling through her. Angela raised her eyes to look at his masculine beauty as he reclined on the cushion.

His head rested against the loveseat, his eyes closed, a ghost of a smile on his sculpted lips while his fingers tangled in her hair. "Ahh… *ma Cherie.*"

He shut the vibrator off, keeping his hand on her head for another heartbeat. She sucked once more. His body jerked before he slipped out of her mouth.

"*Cherie, mon diu,* it's too much. Your hot mouth gives me so much pleasure."

Angela slumped forward between his legs. She rested her cheek on his muscular thigh. *Where are these tears coming from? Why am I crying?* He'd used her in the worst possible way. The vibrator was for his pleasure, and then he'd caressed her cheek and called her *Cherie,* French for darling. He'd never called her by such an endearment. She could understand pussycat and wildcat, but not *Cherie.*

"Stand up, pussycat, and I'll remove your toy." She lay between his legs, unable to move. His palm touched her cheek and lifted her face. "Tears. Did I hurt you?" He sounded concerned. Lifting her from the floor, he carried her to the bed.

"No more, please. You've punished me enough."

"Shh." He nuzzled her hair and kissed her lips. "My beautiful Angela, this is not punishment." He laid her on the bed and gently removed the vibrator. "*Cherie,*" he whispered, and threw the vibrator. It thumped against the wall before it fell to the floor. "I'll be right back, *ma Cherie.*"

She closed her eyes, and more tears seeped between the lashes. In all the time she'd been here, she took what he dished out. She knew he was angry with her, and he had every right to his anger, but now to use an endearment while he treated her like a common whore… It was too much.

WHEN ANDRE SAW her on her knees, resting her head against his thigh, he let go of all his anger. His need for revenge washed away from his soul. Andre walked into his dressing room, grabbed a pair of gray lounge pants, and put them on. He hurried into the en suite and pulled a washcloth and a towel from the shelf. While he soaked the cloth, he thought, *Why was she crying? Did I hurt her? I've never wanted to hurt her or see her cry.* She'd stood up to the worst of his anger. She'd kept her dignity even when he'd done his utmost to bring her down. He hurried back into the bedroom.

Angela lay on the bed. Her hair had come loose of the satin tie and was now a mass of jet-black ringlets across the blue satin pillow. She'd flung her arm over her eyes, the diamond choker still around her neck and her legs pressed together. She hadn't covered herself.

"Would you like a drink?"

She physically stiffened at his words. Keeping her forearm over her eyes, she gave a barely there shake of her head.

Fear gripped his soul, and he felt sick at his actions. *I love her.* He'd kicked the vibrator away, determined to throw it out. Never to treat her in such a terrible way ever again, caring only for his pleasure.

"*Cherie,* I brought you a towel... Please let me..." He moved her legs. "*Mon Dieu,*" he gasped, "the cool cloth will soothe you." He gently lay the cloth on her swollen mound. "I'm so sorry, *Cherie.*"

He'd never used a woman so badly, and he was full of regret and self-loathing. What was it about her that drove him so? Her rejection, the way she'd used him, her defiance—What was it? *That she planned on leaving you.* He walked away from relationships and never looked back, but with her, he couldn't seem to stop himself.

"*Cherie*, let me get you some champagne and more of the chocolates you like." *Anything to make up to you for my boorish behavior.*

She moved her arm from her face. The tears had dried, but the look of accusation in her eyes killed him. "Are you trying to make me forget the way you've treated me? Then let me go. I want to leave this place and never set eyes on you again."

"No!" he shouted, and even the walls vibrated. "Please rest. Is the towel helping?"

She didn't answer.

"Please, is it helping you?"

She nodded.

"*Qui*, I'll get another." Andre held back a shudder when he saw how vicious he'd been with the vibrator. He brought her another towel and placed it between her legs, then he reclined on the bed next to her.

He scrubbed his hand through his hair before he turned to look at her. He reached for the cover at the foot of the bed and brought it up to her chin. "Please calm down, and then we can talk. I'm so sorry. I'll never again touch you in anger."

"You'll never again touch me. I don't trust you, and I want to leave this place. Let me go home."

"Rest now, and then we can talk." He cradled her in his arms until she fell asleep. Then he gently laid her against the pillows. He removed the diamonds from her neck and laid them on the nightstand. Later that night, Andre paced the floor of his office. He'd fallen in love with Angela, but he'd treated her so badly, he couldn't even look at her, wanting only to beg her forgiveness.

When he saw the money she'd hidden, he lost his mind. She was going to leave him. He would do anything to right this terrible wrong. She wanted to go, and he would honor her decision. He paced the floor of his bedroom, grateful that she slept. Tomorrow, he would… For the first time in his life, he was at a loss. He didn't know what he would do.

Andre stood at the bedroom window. He watched as night gave way to the dawn. Streaks of deep blues mixed with pinks lit the sky when Angela stirred in the bed. How could he have been so brutal? He walked over to her. "How do you feel, *ma cherie*? I would beg your forgiveness… I doubt you will ever find it in yourself to forgive me."

She smoothed her hair from her face. "I want to go home today, now. Perhaps in the beginning, you had a legitimate reason for what you did. I allowed you your justice, and you've satisfied whatever misbegotten thoughts of revenge you had. But now I am finished! I won't submit to you ever again."

He let out a long breath and in a husky whisper, he said, "Go shower and dress… I'll honor your wishes. My plane and flight crew will be at your disposal to take you wherever you wish to go. James will drive you to the airport and accompany you." *Goodbye, mi amor.* He brushed his knuckles against her soft cheek before bending to kiss her lips.

Angela pulled away, and he turned from her. With his head bowed, he walked out of the room. He'd fallen in love with her. His heart ached at his cruelty.

CHAPTER 9

*A*ngela sat up in the four-poster bed and stared at Andre's back. His lounge pants rode low on his hips, and the muscles across his back rippled as he walked out of the room.

She shouted, "That's it? No remorse for treating me like a, a whore. Using my body for your own pleasure. You're a mean man, despicable in your treatment of me. I hate you." *Ugh, he is such a miserable bastard.*

She threw the pale-blue comforter off and swung her legs out of the bed. Angela stood for a moment waiting for pain or an ache, but she realized she wasn't sore at all and walked across the Persian rug to the en suite. Her sex swelled from how excited she'd been and not from any damage he'd caused her with the vibrator.

A smile lifted the corners of her lips, and her lids drifted down over her eyes for a second. She'd lost count of how many orgasms she had, the decadent pleasure so unbelievable. Angela soaked in Andre's luxurious tub once more. At home, she didn't have a big bath and certainly not a whirlpool.

While she soaked, Danielle brought her coffee and a pastry. When Angela finished, she stood and picked up a big white fluffy towel, warm from the heating rack. She wrapped it around her body, enjoying the warmth.

She used the hairdryer that Andre had bought for her, along with styling products. One day last week, he'd arranged for a stylist to come to the apartment. Massage, manicure, and pedicure, the woman even trimmed her hair. Angela laughed at the memory. The stylist trimmed the ones between her legs as well.

Now, with the towel wrapped around her, she went into the bedroom and stopped short. A gasp escaped her when she saw her suitcase opened at the foot of his bed. She hurried over and saw her cell phone on top of one of her black dresses. Moving the phone out of the way, she picked up her Chanel black wool dress and found her cotton bra and panties. Taking them from the case, she put on her underwear and the black dress. The fabric slipped over her body, feeling some comfort in again wearing her own clothes. Since her phone was powered off, she slipped it into a side pocket of her case.

Once Angela dressed, she walked to the dressing room and grabbed the clothes he'd given her—hangers and all. Angela took them and dumped the exquisite designer outfits on the floor at the foot of the bed. Then she gathered the sheer robes, the lace bras, and thongs, especially the thong with the pearl crotch, as well as the jewelry he'd bought her. She threw them all on top of the pile of clothes on the floor.

Her first thought after that was to shred the sheets, but she wouldn't act like the vindictive shrew he'd accused her of being. Angela took a deep breath and slowly let it out as she bent by the suitcase. She found her own low-heel black Gucci pumps tucked in a side pocket of her suitcase. She slipped them on and zipped the case closed. Without a second glance, holding her head high, she squared her shoulders and walked out of his bedroom.

James stood in the hall. He stepped forward. "Madame Lombardo, please allow me to carry your suitcase." Angela handed it over to the butler.

"One more thing, Madame, Monsieur Bourbon requests you wear the mink coat. It is bitterly cold out today."

She hesitated as he held the coat open for her to slip into. She'd leave it on the plane, wanting nothing of his to remind her of that dirty bastard and the time she'd spent in Paris, at his mercy, in his home. *I was lost in lust. That was all this was.*

Andre's Mercedes waited in the street in front of the mansion. Grey smoke puffed up from the exhaust. It was indeed freezing outside. A uniformed driver stood at the back passenger door. When she stepped out of the house, the driver opened the back door for her. James brought her luggage to the trunk while she slid into the backseat. Then James sat in the front passenger seat next to the chauffeur.

She settled against the leather seat in the back of the limousine, looking directly ahead, not caring to see if Andre watched or thinking about his lips, his hands... nothing. They drove to the airport in silence. She wanted to go home to her cozy townhouse.

Angela boarded the sleek white plane and sat in the luxurious cabin of Andre's private jet. Giorgio's jet was similar, but his was matte black. Two hours later, Angela peered out the window, waiting to land in Palermo. *Why are men such over-sensitive babies? He and Ricardo won, I lost the battle, and it seems the war, but I can move on. What is that bastard's problem?* Once the jet touched down, and they taxied on the runway, stopping near the terminal, Angela unbuckled her seatbelt.

James approached. "Madame, there's a car waiting for you on the tarmac. Do you wish me to accompany you?"

"No, I can manage quite well." She stood. The white mink

laid on the seat next to her and that was where it would stay. Angela left everything that would remind her of the miserable Frenchman behind. She wanted to forget him and all that he'd done to her. The only thing she wanted was to be home and cease to remember the terrible ordeal she'd been through at the hands of Andre Bourbon. The Frenchman thought he'd earned the right to use her as his plaything.

When she debarked, she slid into the backseat of the limousine that waited on the tarmac. She spoke to the driver in her Sicilian dialect, "I assume you have the address of where I wish to go."

"*Si, signora, subito.*"

Angela carried her own suitcase up the stone steps of her townhome. At the front door, she entered her code for the keyless entry system. The sound of the latch opening was a welcome relief. She wanted to get in bed and sleep for a week.

She was home.

She turned off the ringer on her landline and disconnected the answering machine. That first night, she slept so peacefully, a dreamless night. In the morning, when she got up from the bed, her head spun, and she had to sit back down. The slightest hint of nausea attacked her stomach. She had arranged for her housekeeper to bring her groceries and tidy up. There wasn't much to do other than dust.

Angela was away less than three weeks. She didn't want to turn on her cell phone or check her voicemail. She didn't like computers and kept off social media. She would have to talk with Giorgio, but what would she say? There was still the matter of Ricardo. Everyone must know what she'd done to Ricardo and Liz. The stock situation... all of it... She would have to go talk with her brother and sister-in-law if they would allow her into their home.

What would she say to them? She was reckless and

deceitful because—why? Why was she so malicious? Angela spent the day at home, not bothering to do anything but relax and sleep. *Why am I so tired? Palermo and Paris are in the same time zone. Tomorrow will be soon enough to think about what I'm going to say to my brother.* She picked out an old comfy cotton nightgown from her dresser, banishing thoughts of Andre and the sheer robes he'd given her to wear, and went to bed early that night.

Angela stayed home for a couple of days, not bothering to go out. She was exhausted from how Andre had treated her in Paris. Now that she was home, she could recuperate and gather her strength. Her housekeeper brought her a pot of homemade minestrone soup, which she barely ate. Angela made herself some pasta, but then she ate mostly fruits. Food that was easy to digest, nothing too heavy or rich.

Bored with the self-confinement she'd imposed on herself, Angela decided she'd go to her brother, Giuseppe DiMarco, and her sister-in-law to try to clear up the mess she'd caused. She called her brother and arranged to meet him at his house. Her stomach was queasy, but nothing that a few crackers or a breadstick wouldn't help to settle.

Giuseppe, a tall man with a receding hairline and a salt and pepper short beard, had the same black eyes as she and most of the DiMarcos.' He was in his early-sixties and had a slight paunch. Her sister-in-law Maria was several years older than Angela; she was an elegant, quiet-spoken woman with wheat-colored hair, a few inches taller than Angela.

They both greeted her when their housekeeper announced her at their palazzo. Her sister-in-law was a little better at expressing her feelings than her brother. He only blustered and shouted. Angela knew they were both angry with her. They'd almost refused her coming over. She'd pleaded with them on the phone, and now she asked if they would let her talk first, so she could try to smooth things over.

This was the home Angela grew up in when her parents were alive and before she married Salvatore. Now the home belonged to Giuseppe and Maria. They sat in the formal living room of the grand palazzo. Ceiling-to-floor, dusky-pink velvet drapes covered the many windows of the room. Gold-fringed tiebacks held the drapes open to let in the natural light. The cream-and-white marble floor was polished to a high shine, and accent Persian rugs were scattered on the floor by the rose-colored sofas. The same grand piano she learned to play on sat in a corner of the room.

Angela looked at her brother. She hoped the remorse she felt came across as she said, "I don't know why I did all those terrible things. Ricardo and Liz must hate me, and I can't blame them, but please try to see if we can patch this up and be a family again."

Her brother turned to her, his eyes flashing in anger, and then he took a shuddering breath before he shouted at her, "You've been stubborn from the beginning. This animosity goes back to when Sal died." He shook his head and spoke in a calmer voice, "Yes, I know you lost a husband, and Giorgio lost a father, someone to guide him." He pounded his chest with a fist. "I lost my best friend and my brother-in-law. I meant what I said about guiding Giorgio, but you only heard and saw what you wanted."

Angela held back tears, trying for composure. She took in a slow breath and let it out just as slowly before she could talk. "I know everything you say is true. I was too young to realize and even though that's no excuse, I was devastated. I found myself a young widow with a child. I wanted to be part of the company that you and Salvatore built, but you wouldn't allow a woman in—"

"I can't believe you've held this anger in you all these

years. It was a terrible time for all of us, you and Giorgio, but we tried to unite as a family. It seems you were waiting to hurt Ricardo." He raised his voice, shouting, "My son never did anything to you." Giuseppe stood. "We'll find a way to put this behind us… It may not be as easy as we want, but we'll all try. Rico and Liz are together again; their son Tony is a happy child for all that his early years were spent without a father."

Those words dug into Angela's heart. She was the reason Ricardo didn't know Liz was pregnant four years ago. *I tried to convince Liz that Ricardo wanted her to have an abortion. I offered her money, telling her it came from Ricardo…Giorgio grew up without a father, but Giuseppe was good to him. Treating him just like he did his own sons. I knew that, and yet I tried to destroy Ricardo.*

When Angela went home that night, she found a bouquet of flowers on her doorstep. *Agh, why can't he take the hint? I keep refusing his lousy flowers. Why is he so stubborn?* She lifted the bouquet, not bothering to look at the arrangement. She took them out back and threw them into the trash can.

Exhausted from all the tension with her brother, Angela didn't need to deal with Andre. She climbed the steps to the living room, planning to sit on the couch for a moment. The chime of the grandfather clock woke Angela up. She glanced at the clock in her living room. It was two a.m., and she was starving, so she went into the kitchen and made herself a panino of prosciutto and drizzled some olive oil on it. She cut a wedge of provolone and took a few green olives from the container.

Her emotions were raw, and she knew her brother was right. After she ate, she went to her bedroom and crawled under the covers. She fell into a deep sleep, sleeping late in the morning. Again, she spent the day at home, not caring to do much of anything. Her doorbell rang and when she answered, a courier delivered a package from a jewelry store. She asked the courier to wait while she opened the package. A beautiful diamond bracelet laid on a blue velvet bed. She snapped the lid closed, put the box back into the pouch, and gave it to the courier. "Return it to Mr. Bourbon," she said. She wouldn't accept his gift.

The following day, another courier arrived with the most expensive bottle of her favorite perfume. She returned that as well. The hazelnut chocolate truffles went back, the same as all the other gifts. She wanted nothing from the dirty bastard. First, he wanted revenge; now he wanted to clear his conscience. *Let him stew in his guilt.*

In the morning, she turned on the ringer of her landline and her answering machine. She kept her cell phone turned off. Just before *pranso,* her phone rang. "*Pronto,*" she said into the receiver.

"Angela, it's Andre." She dropped the phone onto its cradle, disconnecting the call. *Why can't he leave me alone?*

Her phone rang again. She walked away. The answering machine came on, and she heard Andre's angry voice. "I know you're there. Pick up. Angela, please I must talk to you. Please." She walked from the room. The begging sounded good… Perhaps if he groveled, I would consider. What am I saying? There is nothing to consider. I don't love him.

CHAPTER 10

$\mathcal{A}$ndre sat at his desk, staring at nothing, thinking of that little witch. She hung up on him and then wouldn't pick up the phone. The day he'd sent her away, he'd stood at his study window and watched her as she walked out of his mansion. She'd never turned to look back. She'd held her head up and walked out of his life. He loved her and would honor her decision to go.

He'd gone into his bedroom after watching his limousine pull away with Angela. She'd left the clothes he'd bought her in a pile on the floor by the foot of the bed. His first reaction was anger—but that lasted a second. He knew she had every right to be angry with him. Then when James returned, carrying the white mink coat, his heart sank—he deserved her scorn.

His bedroom, the house, for that matter, felt empty without her. He'd asked Danielle to hang Angela's clothes back in the dressing room wardrobe. That was a mistake. Her fragrance lingered—orange blossom and her unique scent mingled. He craved her taste on his tongue.

Andre hadn't slept in days. He hadn't shaved or dressed,

other than lounge pants and a t-shirt. He sat in his study, drinking to excess. His chef made him tempting meals, but all he did was drink his expensive whiskey straight from the bottle. No matter how much he tried to drink himself into oblivion, his thoughts always returned to Angela. How could he have fallen in love with that lying, manipulative witch?

If he could beg her forgiveness for his crass behavior, he would. He couldn't sleep in his bed or go swimming. The dining room and his office were unbearable. Wherever he turned, his mind conjured up visions of Angela. He had to get away. There were too many memories of her.

He paced the length of his bedroom, stopping now and then to take a swig from the bottle. He smirked, thinking she'd hidden a very desirable body under her black mourning clothes.

Andre closed his eyes, and she was there. She was every-where. Her scent filled his head, and the taste of her kisses lingered on his tongue. He strolled into the en suite and looked in the mirror. Bloodshot eyes stared back at his unkept self. He had to sober up, so he turned on the faucet and splashed cold water on his face. Then he dunked his head under the faucet.

Andre towel dried his hair and ran his hand along his jaw. The thick, dark-blond growth needed to be shaved. He sighed. He didn't want to do anything. Andre forced himself to make a thick, creamy lather with his shaving soap and proceeded to shave.

Andre didn't need to do anything if he didn't want to. His companies had loyal and top-notch employees. All he needed to do was check in from time to time. Maybe he should look at the proposal for the new venture. That would keep him busy. *Keep my mind off that Sicilian temptress.*

He'd asked James where she'd had his pilot take her, but he knew, even before James told him; she'd gone home to

Palermo. He sent her bouquets of flowers daily, three dozen red roses. His note read *one dozen for each glorious week you were with me.* Did she read the note? She'd returned the roses. He bought her a diamond bracelet, not a line bracelet but an intricate thick, diamond bracelet. That came back; the perfume, and the chocolates were also returned. He called her to tell her he'd given her back the two million dollars, but she'd hung up on him before he could say anything. He'd flung his phone across the room with such force, it made a dent in the wall before it bounced to the floor.

What would she say when she found out he had deposited ten million dollars into her account? He would have to wait before he tried to beg her for her forgiveness. *Did she ever care about me, or was it all her deceitful lies and manipulative nature?*

His private cell phone rang. Glancing at the screen, he saw it was from Angela's landline.

"Hello—"

"Are you trying to clear your conscience? Keep your lousy money. I need nothing from you." He heard the click as she disconnected the call.

Now all he wanted to do was get out of Paris—no, get out of Europe. That's when he decided to go to New York and see Jacques.

DiMarco Enterprises' annual board meeting was at the end of January, in New York City. Perhaps he'd talk to her son Giorgio and see if he could find out about Angela, where she was, how she was doing.

~

THE NEXT MORNING, after that call to Andre, Angela ran to the bathroom to be sick. *I must have caught a virus in Paris. I wonder if I can get an appointment to see my doctor today.* She applied a cool towel to her forehead and one on the back of her neck. Her stomach seemed to settle after that. She called the nurse's line for Doctor Conti and secured one of the last appointments for the day.

The nurse thought it would be wise to schedule some labs. So, first thing that morning, before eating, Angela dressed and went to the laboratory. A technician drew blood.

"I need to collect some urine, *Signora* Lombardo. You can use the restroom down the hall. When you finish, leave the sample on the shelf." She handed Angela a sealed container. "I'll send the results to Doctor Conti's nurse.

"Will the doctor have them by the time I arrive for my appointment? I'm his last patient of the day."

"*Si, Signora*, he'll have them later this afternoon."

Angela rolled down the sleeve on her black dress, thanked the woman, and went down the hall to the restroom.

She arrived for her appointment in the big, stone building at six o'clock in the evening. Doctor Conti, an older gentleman with snow-white hair, gave her a thorough examination. Now she was dressed and sitting across from his ornate desk; bookshelves filled with medical books lined the wall behind his desk in his consultation room.

"What?" She laughed in his face. "How can that be? You must be mistaken. They mixed the tests up. Doctor, you've known me for thirty years. I know I've hardly ever been sick, but this must be a mistake. How could it be? How does something like this happen?" She watched him frown at her before he glanced down and shuffled his papers. "See, *Doctore*, even you're confused."

"No, Angela, I'm not confused. I can't understand how you think we didn't double and triple check the results."

"Yes, I know. I received a call and asked to come back to the lab this afternoon, but pregnant? I'm forty-nine years old. It's quite impossible for me to be pregnant. I'll be fifty when I have the baby." She banged her fist onto her lap. "I have a grown son, for goodness sake!"

The doctor sat back in his leather chair and let out a long sigh. Angela refused to believe what he had told her. "Here, take this once a day. They're prenatal vitamins. We'll schedule an ultrasound, but for now… You're healthy, in good shape, and according to your calculations, you missed this month, so I would expect—"

She stood. "*Doctore*, please, I need to think about all this. The news is quite alarming. I have to go home."

At home, she paced the floor of her living room, cursing. "Oh, that bastard, that no good piece of shit. To get me caught like this. I hate him, I hate him!" She spun on her heel. *What to do? I'll call Giorgio*—she stopped short. *What will I say? Your friend Andre Bourbon kidnapped me and… and… now I'm pregnant.* She stopped walking and banged her fist into the palm of her other hand. *That's what I'll do. I'll tell Giorgio that I want to go live in California to help him with his new vineyard.*

She'd called her son in a panic, not knowing what to do. He'd help her get away from Palermo and as far away as she could from Andre. She thought of all the damage she'd done and felt the first pang of remorse. Angela munched on some dry crackers, trying to settle her stomach. If this pregnancy was anything like the one when she carried Giorgio, she could expect morning sickness upon waking up and then again later in the day, usually in the afternoon. Her phone rang, startling Angela out of her thoughts.

"I'm boarding now and should be at your townhome in two hours."

"Okay, thanks. Be careful." By the time Giorgio arrived at her home, she was much calmer and realized there was no need for him to have rushed. He was angry with her over what she'd attempted to do. She calmed down some, thinking that maybe she'd been rash when she'd called her son, pleading with him to come home. She went through her closet while she waited. All she owned were black clothes—even her lounging clothes were black. She ran her finger over the different textured fabric: wool, silk, cashmere… It was time to put the mourning clothes away.

Andre was right in that respect. The color of her clothes wouldn't change how she felt. It was such a tradition in Italy, but more so in the South and especially in Sicily, to wear black for mourning. She would donate the clothes to charity. She went back up to the living room, poured herself a glass of water, and sat on the sofa.

Her doorbell rang, her son Giorgio arrived, and she buzzed him in. Angela met him on the third-floor landing. He looked so much like his father, tall, dark hair, handsome with the most vibrant aqua-blue eyes. She hugged him to her. "Oh Giorgio, I'm sorry to take you away from business, but I needed to talk with you. Come sit in the kitchen. I'll make coffee."

He sat at the rectangular table she'd put a fresh yellow embroidered linen tablecloth on.

"After careful consideration, I'll go to the Napa vineyard."

His head snapped up, and his voice sounded exasperated. "You couldn't tell me this over the phone? You've been gone for weeks with no contact. You sent me that ridiculous text—You missed Christmas, Gianni's wedding—"

She kept her voice calm, not wanting to argue with him. "I don't want to stay here any longer. I needed to talk with you about that and not long distance."

"When you say here, do you mean this house, or Palermo? Are you running away again, Mother? Do you think California is far enough away to forget everything you've done? Where did you go when you disappeared? Your callus behavior—"

"I don't want to talk about it." She moved away from him. *I don't want to tell him I'm pregnant.*

He shook his head and sighed. "After all the trouble you caused, now you don't want to talk about it. Well, then what do you want to talk about?"

"When I arrived home, and you were away, I went to Giuseppe to apologize for my terrible behavior to Ricardo."

"And you think that will make it better?"

She lifted one shoulder in a tiny shrug. "It's a start. Although I doubt Ricardo and Liz will ever forgive me, I am sorry for what I did."

"I don't understand how you could be so manipulative and why you thought you had the right to meddle in such a malicious way."

Angela bowed her head. *He's right.*

Giorgio walked over to her and held her by her shoulders, and she rose. Then he hugged her to him and sighed. "Mom, I want to help you, but can I trust you not to cause any more trouble?"

Who is the parent here? She thought as she patted his cheek.

He held her away from him, his voice with a tinge of wonder as he said, "Your hair is different. Like the mother of my youth."

She hadn't worn her hair in a bun since the day Andre had kidnapped her. She glanced away. "Yes, I've also removed the mourning black that I've worn for twenty-five years."

He gazed at her, a smile playing around his lips. "That dress looks pretty black to me. I hope you'll stop meddling and causing problems. I want to be clear… I'm happy with my life, so I'd be extremely upset if you turned your attention to causing trouble for me."

She stepped back and stretched her neck to look at him. *He looks so much like his father.* "No, Giorgio, you're my son, and I only want the best for you." She patted his hand. "My brother told me you never wanted to become CEO of DiMarco Enterprises. He offered you the opportunity, and you turned it down."

Giorgio's tone was patient. She felt as if he were talking to a child. "I told you that years ago. Had you listened to me, you would have known."

"*E*, sometimes mamas think they know best."

He shook his head and sighed. "When do you want to leave for California?"

"Right away. And Giorgio, I don't want anyone to know where I am." *Especially not your friend Andre Bourbon.*

His brows came together in a deep frown. "I know you, Mom. What are you hiding? I'm sure there's much more you're not telling me."

She shrugged a shoulder and tipped her head. *Oh yes, but not yet.* "You always think the worst."

"With good reason. I feel you can take charge of the project at the vineyard. It'll give you something to do where you can use your managerial skills. I'll notify the architect."

"I'd like to stop in Milan for a few days, and maybe New York, do some shopping, and then go to California. I can go alone. I know you have appointments and obligations. My brother said I can use one of DiMarco Enterprises' jets, so I'd like to leave tomorrow."

He kissed her. "I'm going home now, and I'll make the arrangements. You can stay at the mansion. Try to behave."

"Oh you, who is the parent here, you or me?" She listened to his laughter as he walked down the steps.

Angela sighed and decided that she shouldn't put off talking with Ricardo and Liz. She wanted to take the first step in fixing the mess she'd caused.

When she dialed her nephew's cell phone number, she held her breath, hoping he wouldn't answer the call. But he picked up after the first ring. *"Pronto, Zia Angela."*

"Hello, Ricardo. If you're free and willing to see me… I'd like to come over today before dinner and talk with you and Liz."

Angela felt the blast of arctic air in his voice as he said, "We're home." Then he disconnected the call.

Ricardo's palazzo was about ten minutes from her townhome. Angela stopped at a toy store before going to her nephew's home. She hadn't seen Ricardo and Liz since the welcome party Giuseppe had thrown for all the friends and relatives stranded in New York City by the blizzard last December. Giorgio and her nephew Lorenzo DiMarco had avoided the blizzard when they flew to California before the airports closed.

At that party, Angela learned that Ricardo and Liz had eloped during the blizzard. Their son Tony, Liz's friend Anna Carducci, and Ricardo's PA Massimo were with them during that time. Another pang of remorse touched Angela. She'd been so malicious to Liz, telling her that Ricardo left her for another woman and how he didn't want her or the child she carried. She had brought an envelope full of cash for Liz when they met at a coffee shop near Ricardo's penthouse. Telling her that Ricardo wanted Liz to have an abortion… She was so cruel to Liz. Thank God Liz didn't listen to her. Angela's hand drifted down to her belly. *How could I have been so vicious and heartless to Liz?*

Angela pulled into the driveway of her nephew's palazzo. She slipped out of her red Fiat and picked up the beautifully wrapped gift she'd bought for the little boy. She rang the doorbell, and Rosaria, Ricardo's housekeeper, opened the door. *"Buon pomeridgio Signora, entre."*

"Grazie."

"Signore DiMarco asks you to please wait in the living room. He'll be right down."

She sat on the sofa and waited. Ricardo walked in. He had

the same DiMarco coloring as she, with jet-black hair and black-as-night eyes. He was a tall man, with chiseled features. Right now, his expression was cold and unwelcoming. "Hello, I'm surprised you wanted to see me. I thought after all the trouble you caused and then you disappeared, you wanted nothing to do with your family."

He doesn't know that Andre kidnapped me or... don't think of that. "I want to apologize. I've no words that can let you know how badly I feel about my behavior to you and Liz. I was hoping to see Liz—"

His voice thundered, "After all of your vicious lies and your betrayal, you expect me to allow you near my wife and son... I don't think so. You've apologized, now go." He lifted his arm and pointed to the entry.

Angela glanced at the living room entrance, hoping to see Liz, before she held out the brightly wrapped package containing a police car. "I brought this for your son, Tony."

He glanced at the gift, but other than that, he didn't take it, so she placed it back on the seat next to her purse. "Rico, I know I did some terrible things to you, and all you did was try to help me, but you must understand—"

"Understand what?" he shouted at her. "You have been vicious and mean spirited. How long did you plan this treachery? Using your friend Andre to buy stocks in the Contessa cruise line and setting him and Liz up with those photos. You manipulated Liz and me. I believed your lies, that the photos were of Liz." His hand cut through the air. "Agh, I can't even look at you."

"I know I deserve everything you're saying. I won't even try to justify all the mess I caused." *You should only know how I'm paying for this.* Angela stood on shaky legs. "You're right. I know we can never be a close family again. I hope that one day, you can forgive me and that I can tell Liz how sorry I am."

"My wife has a big and generous heart, so she may forgive you but expect nothing from me."

"Okay, I've said what I came to say." Angela picked up her purse from the sofa and walked out of the room. She didn't wait to be led out of her nephew's palazzo. She got into her car and drove the short distance back to her townhome.

Whether her nephew accepted her apology no longer mattered. She'd made the effort and explained her behavior. She knew she'd been irrational, but at the time... well, she thought they had pushed Giorgio to the side.

ANGELA FLEW to Milan for a day of shopping, the mecca of Italian fashion. She always enjoyed shopping at the flagship stores of her favorite Italian designers. This was the first time in such a long time that she'd been shopping for clothes other than the mourning black. Then reality sank in. Soon, she'd need maternity clothes.

The styles had certainly changed from the last time she needed to wear such clothing. She was happy to indulge in a whole new wardrobe. Dresses, suits, with pants and skirts, with loose-fitting waistbands. She'd need blouses and lingerie, certainly none of the things Andre had made her wear. *Why did I think of him? Oh... he woke up your hedonistic nature...*

Her hand moved to her stomach. Already she felt uncomfortable with anything tight on her waist. Her purchases were delivered to DiMarco Enterprises' private jet. Later that day, she flew on to New York City. Angela made use of the luxurious jet's master suite, sleeping all the way. When she arrived in New York, she went directly to her hotel suite. Her pregnancy made her tired, so she spent a day resting before shopping along Fifth Avenue.

Ricardo was in Sicily, but she avoided his Fifth Avenue

penthouse and the possibility of meeting any friends. She kept to herself, not wanting to tell anyone that she was pregnant. She had the most difficult time even thinking of the word—pregnant. How? Not the physical that she knew. Andre used her, and she loved his erotic skill, dreaming of him night and day. She should be a grandmother and not a mother again. She slept, ate, and craved Andre.

She spoke with the overseer at the Napa vineyard, and he told her that Giorgio had notified him of her arrival, and he'd had the owner's suite at the mansion prepared for her. She thanked him, but she preferred to stay in one of the cottages on the property. He seemed to like that, telling her they were much more comfortable than the immense house. She would stay in one of the smaller cottages while she organized the renovations on the mansion and all the work on the restaurant.

When she arrived, exhausted from the shopping and travel, she spent a few days resting. She now took extra care to rest and eat right. Angela went for long walks in the morning, enjoying the California sunshine. She took the vitamins each morning that her doctor in Palermo had prescribed. Angela found an ob-gyn with top-notch credentials. She'd prefer to give birth back home in Sicily, but she knew she would need a local doctor.

She'd had two miscarriages after Giorgio, so she worried about this baby. The doctor at the time of her last miscarriage said it was likely because she was so young when she'd had Giorgio. Her body would recuperate, but Sal never wanted to take a chance after the miscarriages.

Andre had to escape his Paris home.

He flew to New York City, but that was no better. He

drank all day and into the early morning hours, stumbling into bed only to lie awake, staring at the ceiling, thinking of that Sicilian witch. Andre stayed in his robe, or if he thought to change, he'd throw on a pair of lounge pants. He hardly ate, and he was the worst company to his brother Jacques. He could have helped his brother, but he was useless to anyone right now. Thoughts of that deceitful witch, no... tempting seductress, consumed him.

He hated her... he loved her... he needed her. Andre knew what he'd lost with his callous behavior and thoughts of revenge. He lost the love of his life. He'd never treated a woman the way he treated her. Andre never forced a woman to have sex with him... but Angela had found a way into his heart... When he learned how she'd used him, his rage consumed him, blinding him to all else.

He never contacted Giorgio and towards the end of February, James came into the study where Andre had spent the night drinking. "Sir, I thought you'd like to know that Giorgio Lombardo married on Valentine's Day in Las Vegas. Madame Lombardo was at the wedding."

He growled at James, "I need a haircut."

"Yes sir. I'll have your stylist come to the apartment, perhaps a shave and massage?"

"Yes, let me know when he gets here... Was there a photo?"

"Yes, to accompany the headline, followed by a brief statement. Shall I find the article on the internet?"

"No."

After his stylist left, Andre attempted to rejoin humanity and dressed in something more than a t-shirt and lounge pants. The spacious four-bedroom apartment with a gourmet kitchen and a gym was closing in on him. *I'll have to beg and grovel more than I did. I have to win her back. I love her.*

Andre walked into the kitchen for coffee and found his

brother at the table. Jacques was as tall as Andre, with the same athletic build. "Hello, big brother. Will you grace me with your presence?"

"I know that I've been a bear and the worst company, but I won't apologize."

Jacques tipped his head to one side. "You've been rude to James, snapping and yelling at him... Do you want to talk about your problem?"

"Hell no—let's talk about why you're getting a divorce."

"I'll say that I came home unexpectedly from the office to find my wife in our bed with our next-door neighbor."

"I'm sorry. So, she's not contesting the divorce?"

"She's getting a fabulous settlement she's thrilled with and won't fight me on this... They've moved in together."

"I don't know what to say to you other than good riddance to her."

"I was numb in the beginning, more so for how blind I'd been to what was going on right under my nose. She told me they'd had a sexual relationship for two years. She blamed me for being a workaholic." Jacques shrugged a shoulder. "I know I am, so... I can't blame her."

"It's better that you can move on, and she can be happy with her new significant other." *I wish I could forget Angela and move on.*

ON A BITTERLY COLD, snow-covered day at the beginning of March, his private cell phone rang. Few people had that number, so he glanced down at the screen and saw the call was from Angela. *Am I dreaming?*

"Hello, *ma belle.*"

"I need to talk with you. Can you meet me?"

"Yes, where are you?"

The connection was silent for so long; he thought the call had dropped.

And then she said, "I'm in California at my son's Napa Valley vineyard."

He glanced down at the time display on his phone. "I can be there later today. Tell me exactly—"

"I'll text you the address."

"Okay. See you soon."

Andre hurried to his bedroom and threw some clothes into his suitcase. He asked James to have his jet ready and for the pilot to file a flight plan to Napa Valley. "You know the drill. I'll need a car and driver at my disposal."

"Yes, sir, shall I pack a bag for myself?"

"No, I'll go alone. You hold down the fort here. You've done a great job taking care of everything, including my brother and me. I know I've been short tempered recently." Andre snapped closed his suitcase. "Do you know where my brother is?"

"He's in the home office, sir."

Andre hurried to the office and found Jacques at his desk. "I'm going to California; I don't know for how long."

His brother glanced up from his computer, his eyes narrowing. Giving a slight nod, he said, "The reason you've drunk half the liquor cabinet… and may I add, your boorish behavior has finally called?"

Andre nodded and smirked before he said, "You, little brother, know me so well. I've left her alone as she requested, so I have no idea why she's called now."

"I guess you'll find out soon enough. Knowing you, your jet is probably on the runway waiting for you."

"Yes, it is."

Jacques stood, giving his brother a hug. "Be safe."

～

ANGELA WORRIED over what to wear, not wanting the slight baby bump to be the first thing he saw. She chose a casual powder-blue floral silk designer dress she'd bought in Milan. The dress was loose fitting, with tiny iridescent buttons down the bodice. It was comfortable and mid-length, with a ruffle at the hem. She wasn't big, but it was noticeable at certain angles.

She had plenty of time to think of what she would say to Andre when he arrived.

Her doctor's appointment earlier today compelled Angela to call him. While looking at the ultrasound monitor, she let out her breath and let go of all her anger. She'd wanted to keep the pregnancy from him, but after the ultrasound today, she knew it would be unfair to do so. She had to let Andre know he could add daddy to his title. Angela called him even before she'd walked out of her doctor's office.

Now, from the large bay window in the living room, Angela watched as a sleek black limousine glided to a stop in front of the cottage. Andre emerged from the backseat. She hurried to meet him at the entrance to the two-story home, swinging open the front door before he rang the bell. Angela gazed up at him. He looked haggard, thinner, but his blond hair was neatly trimmed, and he was freshly shaven. The scent of his cologne drifted through the midafternoon California air.

Angela took a breath of the spicy scent, and her nipples tightened. She hadn't expected that reaction, but why not? She had the most erotic dreams of him. Sometimes waking up panting and reaching over for him before she remembered she was alone in her bed. She blamed it on the pregnancy, positive her hormones caused that reaction. Angela fought the thought that it could be anything but the fact that he'd awakened her sensual appetite, and not that she'd fallen in love with him.

He held her shoulders and brushed his lips against her right cheek and then her left. "*Cheri*, it's so good to see you… Is it possible?" He held her from him. "Yes, you've grown more beautiful. You're glowing."

She failed miserably at ignoring her body's reaction to him. "Come in." She turned on her blue high-heel pumps, trying to calm herself, and led the way down the light and airy hall, making sure to walk a step ahead of him. "Would you like a coffee or perhaps something stronger?" *You're going to need it.*

"Coffee, yes ma petite beauty… I'm delighted that you're not wearing black, and your lovely hair is loose and flowing down your back. I'm most surprised to hear from you."

"I'm sure you were… surprised… that is." She opened the door to the study, a room much more intimate than the formal living room. The shutters were open to let in the natural California sunlight. "Come sit on the couch. I made the espresso earlier. Let me get it." Then she smiled and glanced at him through the fringe of her lashes. "You won't drug my coffee now, will you?"

Angela saw him tense for a moment before he ran his fingers through his blond hair.

She couldn't help but laugh at his reaction.

Then he said in all seriousness, "I'm sorry for that terrible misdeed. My anger overcame reason. You can check—"

"Andre, I'm teasing you." She flipped her hair over her shoulder. "I'll be right back."

It didn't take her long to return, holding the tray so it camouflaged the slight roundness of her belly. She put the tray down on the coffee table and handed him his drink. Angela went to sit on the wing chair opposite the couch. She crossed her ankles and leaned forward. "I may as well come right to the point… I'm pregnant." Her satisfaction came with the sound of his cup rattling on the saucer.

Surprise etched his handsome features. "How far along are you, that you're just telling me now?"

With a slight shrug of one shoulder, she said, "I've known since January. I went to my doctor in Palermo thinking I had a stomach virus… only to learn—"

His voice boomed, "It's March, so you were going to keep this from me to punish me?"

"No, not as punishment, but there's more—"

He rose from the couch and came over to her. Taking her hand, he knelt by her side. "What is it, *Cheri?* Are you well? The baby?" He kissed the palm of one hand and then the other. "Whatever you need, I'll get it for you."

"Andre, please." She rose from her seat, smoothing the floral light-blue silk fabric over her stomach.

His eyes rounded as they roamed over her belly. Ever so gently, his big hand reached out to touch the slight bump. "This is my baby growing in you," his French-accented voice husky with emotion.

"Babies," she whispered.

"More than one?" he sounded dazed. "Are you all right? I mean healthy. What—"

She suppressed a giggle. "Yes, I'm perfectly healthy, and the twins are thriving. I called you as soon as I found out."

A smile tugged at his lips. "Marry me, now. Today. Look, I'm already on one knee."

Angela took a step back from him. "No, I won't marry you because I'm pregnant."

"That's not the reason I'm asking you to marry me. I want you to know that I've always loved you. Even when I thought it was revenge, it was love. Surely, you must know… I love you."

"How could I know that? The way you treated me, and the way you… you never… anyway, that short time after Christmas, we were lost in lust; that's all it was."

"No, it wasn't lust. We connected. I felt it, and you did too. I know you did."

"I'm not interested in marriage. As the expression goes—Been there, done that."

Andre rose to his feet and held her closer to his powerful body. "Not with me, you haven't." He took a step back, his big hand covering her belly before he said, "These are our babies, and they'll need both of us."

"I'm too set in my ways. I like my independence. I don't want to be married or have a husband telling me what to do or how to act, or where to live."

"We'll live wherever you wish. You, Angela DiMarco Lombardo, *mi amor*, are my home. My life is nothing without you. I love you." He knelt in front of her again, and his arms went around her waist. He tugged her to him, kissing her belly.

The heat of his kisses penetrated the fabric of her dress. She wrapped her hands around his blond head, her fingers clutching at his hair. "Andre, I love you too."

He gazed up into her eyes, and his hands cupped her buttocks. Dragging her closer, he spread more kisses over her belly. "Tell me again. I never grow tired of hearing you say my name."

"Andre, I love you… but I'm not going to marry you."

He sighed and rose to his feet. Taking her hand, he sat on the sofa, tugging her on his lap. "Let's talk about this… I like your independence, although there's no doubt that you've been reckless with it. I don't want a wife who I can keep under my thumb, boss around, tell what to do." He wiggled his brows at her, his hand cupping her hip to drag her closer onto his lap. "I want your independence. I wouldn't mind keeping you under my body, boss you around in bed when we make love."

She shook her head. "I'm too set in my ways to marry. If I want to pick up and go, I can. I don't want to be told—"

"I wouldn't want a brainless wife. I want us to share our lives, raise our children—twins—I'm amazed. I want to be a part of your life and our children's."

"I promised my son I would finish this project, but then… I thought to have the babies in Palermo."

"We can live wherever you want. I'll build you a mansion. I have properties around the world. You say where you want to call home, and I'll follow, *mi amor*."

He brushed his lips over hers, and Angela burned with desire. She turned in his arms and slanted her lips across his, needing the pressure and the heat of his mouth. He slipped his tongue into her mouth, and she almost cried out at the pleasure. The memory of his kisses couldn't compare to this. She felt desire burn in her core and knew she'd agree to whatever he wanted. She broke the kiss, needing to feel his skin, unbuttoning his shirt. Angela slipped her hand over his chest and kissed his neck.

He swelled against her, and Angela's core pulsed with need; she was wet in an instant. He dragged her onto the sofa, and she looped her arms around his powerful neck, pulling him down to her.

"I've missed you, *ma Cheri*; my body is throbbing for you." His hand slid up her leg, pushing the dress aside as he went. Andre reached a bare butt cheek, and he gazed into her eyes. "A thong?"

She whispered, "I didn't have time to find one with pearls."

"*Cheri*." His middle finger stroked the thin fabric covering her mound. "I feel how wet you are for me."

"Yes, Andre, for you… always for you." He kissed her, and she wanted so much more than the gentle sweep of his sculpted lips as she unbuttoned the front of her dress and pressed her breasts to him. "Please don't be gentle."

"Is it safe? I don't want to hurt you."

"It's very safe."

Andre slid the dress off her shoulders and down her arms. He unhooked her bra. "Oh, *ma belle*, your breasts are beautiful." He bent his head to take a nipple into his mouth.

"Yes, Andre, yes." She arched her back, offering her breasts to him.

Andre slipped to his knees between her spread thighs. He placed his hand on the slight bulge of her belly before he bent and kissed every inch of her baby bump. She reached to move her thong to the side, and he slid the scrap of fabric from her body. He slipped it to the floor to rest on top of the dress and bra he'd placed there. "Angela, I need your taste on my tongue."

She slid lower on the couch. "Oh Andre, I need to feel everything you do to me."

He held her gaze as his thumbs glided up and down her seam, exciting her before he spread her. She was on fire and dripping for him, needing his mouth on her, his tongue in her. He touched her ever so slightly and pressed his lips on her before he thrust his tongue into her center. She came in a rush of desire, holding his head to her, yanking on his hair. She couldn't believe how fast it was over, and then he stood with her in his arms. "*Cherie*, I need you."

She looped her arms around his neck. "Yes, my love, take me upstairs to the bedroom… then to Paris, where it all began."

****

Thank you for reading The Frenchman's Revenge

I hope you enjoyed Angela and Andre's story.
The Sea Captain's Redemption is the next book in the DiMarco Empire Series. Read Francesca and Lorenzo's love story here.
Is redemption possible with your friend's younger sister?
Find out in this billionaire age gap, forced proximity romance.
The Sea Captain's Redemption

WHERE TO FIND MY BOOKS

You can find my books at your favorite bookstore, retailer, or library 

Or, you can buy them directly from me at my website https:// CindyReddingAuthor.com

Or,

Cindy's Store https://payhip.com/CindyRedding

If you prefer, please scan this QR Code with your phone

ALSO BY CINDY REDDING

The DiMarco Empire Series

The Sicilian's Betrayal

The Winemaker's Seduction

The Frenchman's Revenge

The Sea Captain's Redemption

Christmas

A Fake Date For Kate

The Christmas Present

The Royals

A Royal Temptation

ABOUT THE AUTHOR

USA TODAY Bestselling Author **Cindy Redding** fell in love with happily ever after when she read her first romance at age twelve. Since then, she has been hooked.

A native New Yorker, Cindy lived on the beach in South Florida and now she lives in Las Vegas, NV, with her husband, of thirty-five years whom she married on Valentine's Day. She has two daughters. Her eldest is named after a heroine in one of Cindy's favorite romances.

Inspired by her travels around the world and her love of Italy, Cindy's sizzling contemporary romance novels come to life with hot men and the strong-willed, independent women who can tame them.

Escape into a world where happily ever after lives.

When she's not writing, you can find her taking long walks in the desert or driving to Disneyland.

Escape into a world where happily ever after lives.
****

Join my newsletter for the free love story of Rose and Leonardo in The Tycoon's Secret Child.

Leonardo Vitale's life changes with one middle of the night phone call. The sinfully handsome hotel tycoon never expected to hear the name Rose Steele again.

Three years ago, Leonardo told Rose he never wanted marriage or children. The sexy grad student walked away from their sizzling passion filled Neapolitan nights, taking her secret back to Texas with her.

Now, an injured Rose wakes to find the man she once

loved sitting by her hospital bed. Leonardo vows to help her recuperate at his home in Sicily so he can bond with his daughter. Can Rose be near him and ignore the memories of their heated nights?

Grab your free copy here.
The Tycoon's Secret Child

ACKNOWLEDGMENTS

I would like to thank Heather Starling for all of her invaluable advice and wonderful insight. I want to especially thank SJS Editorial Services for their quick and thorough editing. You make me shine.

www.ingramcontent.com/pod-product-compliance
Lightning Source LLC
Chambersburg PA
CBHW051230210726
48290CB00003B/892